ABOUT THE AUTHOR

Amber Kell is a dreamer who has been writing stories in her head for as long as she could remember.

She lives in Texas with her husband, two sons, two cats and one very stupid dog. To learn more about her current books or works in progress, check out her blog at http://amberkell.wordpress.com. Her fans can also reach her at amberkellwrites@gmail.com.

Facebook:
http://www.facebook.com/people/Amber-Kell/1772646395

Email:
amberkellwrites@gmail.com

Blog:
http://amberkell.wordpress.com

Twitter:
http://twitter.com/amberkell

Moon Pack

VOLUME ONE

AMBER KELL

Published by Silver Publishing
Publisher of Erotic Romance

If you purchased this book without a cover you should be aware that this book is stolen property. It was reported as "unsold and destroyed" to the publisher, and neither the author nor the publisher has received any payment for this "stripped book."

SILVER PUBLISHING

ISBN 978-1-61495-282-4

Moon Pack 1: Attracting Anthony
Moon Pack 2: Baiting Ben
Moon Pack 3: Courting Calvin
Copyright © 2011 by Amber Kell
Editor: Alison Todd
Cover Artist: Reese Dante

All rights reserved. Except for use in any review, the reproduction or utilization of this work in whole or in part in any form by any electronic, mechanical or other means, now known or hereafter invented, including xerography, photocopying and recording, or in any information storage or retrieval system, is forbidden without the written permission of the editorial office, Silver Publishing, 18530 Mack Avenue, Box 253, Grosse Pointe Farms, MI 48236, USA.

All characters in this book have no existence outside the imagination of the author and have no relation whatsoever to anyone bearing the same name or names. They are not even distantly inspired by any individual known or unknown to the author, and all incidents are pure invention.

Visit Silver Publishing at https://spsilverpublishing.com

ATTRACTING ANTHONY
MOON PACK
BOOK ONE

Anthony goes to the club to start dating again after the death of his lover. He didn't plan on being anyone's mate. The pack alpha had other ideas.

Attracting Anthony

MOON PACK, BOOK 1

AMBER KELL

Published by Silver Publishing
Publisher of Erotic Romance

DEDICATION

I dedicate this to my family who put up with a dusty house and piles of laundry so I can daydream.

CHAPTER ONE

"I can't believe I let you talk me into this," Anthony Carrow muttered to his friend as he looked around the club. It only took him two seconds to think about walking back out, but it took Steven weeks to get a membership to the club and he wasn't going to ruin it for his friend on his first visit.

No matter how much he wanted to.

Anthony felt conspicuous in his leather pants without a shirt, exposing both a pierced left nipple and the brilliant memorial tattoo on his back. It made him feel more naked than he was used to in public. The feeling gradually faded as he realized less people were looking at him than at the young man walking past him with a leash attached to the harness around his cock; a leash clasped in the firm grip of a slim man with silvery hair and a designer suit walking with the smooth grace of werekin.

In reality, with his magical disguise he drew less attention than the dozens of men standing around like they were waiting to take part in the Mr Beautiful pageant.

This is all a horrible mistake. The thought whipped through Anthony's mind in a dizzying fury, setting his nerves strumming so loudly he was surprised the noise didn't echo off the ceiling of the crowded bar.

Panicked, he turned to flee.

A strong grip clamped onto his shoulder holding him in place.

"No escaping. You promised you'd come with me and we both know you need to get out more," said Steven, Anthony's best friend. He watched the provocative pair with the cock leash pass with interested eyes. "You've barely dated since Drew died." He flashed Anthony a sympathetic smile. "You know he'd want you to move on, and although I appreciate your new look, I don't think you did it for me."

He stifled his laughter at Steven's rueful expression. Even though he agreed to accompany his friend to the club, he'd cast a strong suppression spell on his appearance so he wouldn't stand out in the crowd. Anthony didn't need a stampede in his direction on his first night out. Easing into the dating scene gently was the only way he could even think about dating again.

Looking at the clientele he had doubts he was going to find a nice, quiet man to dominate him. He missed his Drew, the strong master who'd been his lover until a heart attack killed him at the age of fifty. Anthony was brokenhearted at the death of his lover, knowing if he'd been home he might have been able to save the other man. Magic did nothing if you weren't there in time to use it. Instead he got home to find his lover dead on their living room floor. An event in his life he knew would stay with him for hundreds of years. Despite what they said about 'time heals all wounds', he knew some things never healed.

The spell he'd cast before coming to the club dulled his gleaming golden hair to a dirty blond and subdued his natural glowing skin to a light bronze. Features heart-stoppingly fine roughened under the weight of magic, changing his normally beautiful features into a pleasing but not memorable face. Everything else he left as nature made it, figuring there would be a lot of fit bodies in the crowd. He worked out every day to keep in shape. Immortality didn't mean a perfect body forever. Due to his spells he was now attractive enough to get a man but not gorgeous enough to overshadow his handsome friend.

However, as much as he wanted to find another person to share his life with, even the thought of dating sent pain ripping through Anthony's chest. Shifters as a group were fit, and as his eyes roamed over the room filled with hot flesh and eager partners all he could think of was that none of them were Drew. Images of his dead lover flashed before his eyes like a moving picture, peeling back his careful indifference to expose a loss so deep it threatened to drown him. Taking a deep breath, Anthony steadied his pulse and forced a reassuring smile to his lips, hoping to stave off the worried expression he saw in Steven's eyes.

Surely three years was long enough. He could do this. He was ready. Maybe if he chanted it a few more times in his head it would become true.

"You aren't asking me to go out more. You dragged me here because you want moral support for your mate hunt. Why you even want to mate is beyond me."

He didn't even want to imagine what would happen if Steven found and lost his mate. Werewolves bonded for life, something that could be good or bad depending on your mate.

"You have something against wolves?" Steven's tone was as challenging as any wild wolf, his eyes feral in the club lights.

Anthony felt an uncomfortable number of gazes turn towards him. Great, just what he wanted; to insult a room full of werekin. A low growl sounded near them. His temper flared but he firmly held it in check. Steven would never forgive him if he crumbled the building and ruined his mate hunting grounds.

"Don't be an idiot. We've been friends forever. If I had a problem with wolves you'd know it by now. I have something against mates."

He felt the surrounding people lose interest in their conversation now that they knew he wasn't a threat. Nothing would be worse than a hunter sneaking onto mating grounds. Anthony had heard of that happening in other cities and the resulting carnage wasn't good. The amount of damage the hunters did was nothing compared to the wolves' retaliation. Towns had lost whole populations in a shifter/human wars.

"Oh don't start that." Steven's voice wasn't unkind but the underlying firmness in his tone told Anthony his best friend was running out of patience. "Just because your lover died doesn't mean you can't find another. Besides, if you don't start dating again your parents will intervene and I've met your parents, they scare the crap out of me."

Anthony shivered at the memory of his parents' matchmaking skills. "Last time they fixed me up with a fairy."

Steven snorted. "I thought you didn't like labels."

"No. He was an actual fairy, you know, from Faeland."

That got Steven's full attention. "What happened?"

Anthony shrugged. "Let's just say it didn't work out." He wasn't going to relive the horrible details of *that* blind date, even for his best friend. Fae princes were a touchy lot. "Anyway, it just proved I wasn't ready to date."

"Fuck it, Tony, it's been almost three years. Even if you don't want a mate there are plenty of hot guys here for a hookup. Hell, even if I don't find the 'one' it'll still be fun shopping." His hungry eyes briefly scanned the crowd before turning to lock eyes with Anthony, his blue eyes filling with compassion. "I understand you lost your soul mate, but you can't go the rest of your life untouched. There are other people out there. If you didn't think it was possible to find someone else you wouldn't have come."

Anthony looked away, blinking rapidly. "I know. I do. It's just hard."

Sighing, he looked around the club. It was an extremely selective club; they didn't let just anyone join. He knew Steven went through a detailed screening process to get a membership, and to have Anthony put on the approved guest list. He was only one of a handful of friends who were on it. He knew he wasn't let in without a screening of his own, a wise move on the club owner's part. It would be all too easy for a hunter to persuade a naïve shifter he was their friend only to wreak havoc once they got inside.

Everywhere Anthony looked there were men and women dancing, drinking, and doing things not usually allowed in public. There were certain advantages to belonging to a private club and, as long as no money exchanged hands between partners, just about anything was allowed between consenting adults.

Tonight it was Steven who was on the hunt.

A werewolf himself, his best friend longed for a mate but was unused to being around others of his kind. Anthony knew it was partly due to the fact that Steven's adoptive parents were full human and unable to understand the complex world of werewolf society. It wasn't for lack of trying, but there were only so many facts you could find on the internet. Werekin didn't give up secrets to people not of their kind or their mates. Steven's parents were sweet and tried hard, but they weren't werewolves.

Anthony wanted to be supportive of his friend's search for a mate, but it was hard. Part of his soul died with Drew and he doubted he'd ever be able to reclaim it. He worried that Steven's hopes of hearts and flowers would end in tragedy like his own love affair. It wasn't better to have loved and lost, it was fucking unfair.

Still, his friend was right, he couldn't stay alone for the rest of his life, and werewolves were known for taking charge in the bedroom. There was nothing he loved more than a firm hand.

With that thought in the forefront of his mind, Anthony looked the room over with new eyes. Instead of trying to keep hidden, he assessed the others to see if any would appeal to either him or to his not-so-discerning friend.

As if catching onto Anthony's thoughts, Steven shared a wicked smile and the pair prowled the room with new intent.

CHAPTER TWO

Silver entered the club from the manager's suite. Thomas, his lieutenant, joined him a moment later.

"It's a good crowd tonight," the wolf said with justifiable pride. Converting the old bar to a safe mating ground for werekin was his idea, a brilliant notion that brought the pack surprisingly large profits.

Silver nodded, giving Thomas a pat on the shoulder. "Profits and memberships are skyrocketing even with our strict entrance restrictions. Both humans and weres like the idea of a forever mate."

"Humans like it because there's too much cheating among their own kind, and weres are genetically coded to search for their other half." Thomas brushed his dark hair back from his face with one elegant hand before giving his boss a reproving look. "You spend too much time alone, Silver. It's time you found a pretty boy and settled down."

The alpha gave a disdainful sniff. "I don't like pretty boys. They need too much attention. Give me a grateful average looking guy any time. Besides, you don't have a mate either."

"Don't change the subject. At least I'm looking. If you really wanted average you could go down to the dance floor, crook your finger, and just grab the first in the stampede."

The alpha wolf's quicksilver eyes flashed amusement. "I said I liked men, not sluts."

Silver restlessly scanned the crowd. Something felt different this evening. There was a tingle in the air, a feeling of magic. The sizzle along his spine warned him of great events hovering in the horizon; a touch of sight descended from his father's line.

He looked towards the dance floor again; making sure everything was flowing smoothly and trying to identify the source of his unease. He saw no fights breaking out, no unwanted touching occurring. Out of habit Silver closed his eyes and took a deep breath, inhaling the scents of the club. His senses first located members of his pack in the dense crowds. A few dozen were there to keep the club moving smoothly, a few others were hunting for mates of their own.

For several minutes he couldn't find anything different or new. Certainly nothing that demanded his attention. Silver was about give up when he smelled it; the scent of a deep, cool forest drifted up to him from the crowd.

Delicious.

Longing filled him. Silver yearned to run under the full moon with rich dirt flying under his clawed feet, to run to the source of that smell. His wolf howled inside him, aching to get out. With a great deal of effort he snapped back to reality.

There wasn't a patch of good running land for miles. Silver closed his eyes and inhaled again, turning his head as the smell drifted past. Unable to help it, the alpha growled.

Someone in the club smelled irresistible.

"What is it?" Thomas asked, his eyes riveted to the expression on Silver's face.

"Don't you smell that?"

"What?"

"Heaven."

Silver's gaze landed on a dark-haired man in tight jeans and a red shirt who swaggered across the floor followed by an unremarkable looking man with dull blond hair, a sweet ass, and a scent from Silver's hottest dreams. The blond's movements were more like a graceful dance than a walk, as if the music itself pushed him across the floor. Without a shirt, he got a good look at the man's smooth tanned skin poured over sleek muscles by a generous creator. The leather pants he wore outlined an ass so fine moisture pooled in Silver's mouth. He had never met Mr Sweetass, but now was the time. It had been too damn long since someone caught his attention.

"I think I just found the Mr Average of my dreams," Silver muttered to his lieutenant. Placing his hands on the wooden banister, he gripped it firmly before flinging himself over the balcony. With their enhanced senses, the dancers fled with seconds to spare. Silver landed on the recently vacated space and strode through the quickly parting crowd to reach the pair now talking in the corner.

The blond faced away from him, giving Silver a view of the tattoo across his upper back. His enhanced sight let him make out the word *Andrew*.

Fury rushed through Silver at the thought of someone else touching the sleek blond. If his splendid smelling man already belonged to another, there would be a murder tonight. No one else could own the man who would soon belong to the alpha.

Mine.

The possessiveness he felt towards this one man took him by surprise, but it didn't stop him from approaching the pair.

"Good evening gentlemen, I'm Silver Moon, the owner of this club. I don't believe I've had the chance to meet you. Are you new members?"

He was rather proud of the fact that he didn't just grab the blond and drag him back to his lair.

See him use restraint.

Both men turned to face him but Silver's eyes locked onto the blond.

The dark-haired man stepped forward, drawing his attention. "Nice to meet you, Mr Moon. I'm Steven Dell, a new member, and this is my friend Anthony Carrow who's come as my guest. I'm trying to talk Tony here into getting back into the dating pool."

"No." The objection burst from his lips without a filter. Silver quickly followed it with a charming smile; he didn't want to scare away the splendid smelling man. Anthony looked up and saw the color of the other man's eyes for the first time. Amazing. This ordinary looking man had extraordinary golden eyes that sparkled like they were made of trapped sunlight.

"Is there something wrong with the men here?" Anthony asked in a smooth tenor, a sweet, dimpled smile lighting his plain face.

Silver cleared his throat to come up with

something plausible. He concentrated on the brunet because he seemed to be the spokesman for them both. "There's nothing wrong with the men here, but you don't want to jump into anything. Why don't you two come back to my table? I'm always happy to get to know new members." Not a complete lie. "And that way the two of you will be able to see everyone and be seen." He darted a glance at the blond. "I'd feel bad if you chose the wrong man on your first foray."

Of course Silver didn't tell the shy Anthony that the wrong man was anyone but him. Instead he held out his hand and bit back a moan when the blond's palm slid across his to shake.

There were many moments in Silver's life that made up special memories, but this one eclipsed them all. It wasn't every day you touch your mate for the first time.

Heat ran up his arm as he took the younger man's hand. Instead of shaking it he lifted it to his lips, placing a soft kiss on the back. This was *the one*. He knew it as well as he knew the phases of the moon and the joy of a good hunt.

"Welcome to my club," he growled.

Steven gave a rueful laugh before

turning to his friend with an easy smile. "Tony, why don't you stay with Silver here, I think I see someone to my taste and I don't want to worry about you."

Silver could've kissed him.

Anthony flashed him a cautious look before turning to his friend. "Are you sure Steve? I know we brought separate cars, but I don't want to abandon you when we've only been here a few minutes.

Someone without enhanced senses wouldn't have heard the tremor in Anthony's voice or felt the nerves pouring off of him in waves. The predator inside Silver wanted to take the sweet boy down like a wounded deer and devour him in the soft comfort of his den.

As it was, it took all his strength to hold back a snarl when Steven placed a soft kiss on his friend's cheek and whispered, "I'll be fine. Call me if you run into any trouble." Silver didn't miss the warning look in Steven's eyes, but he did give the protective werewolf a nod to let him know he would watch out for his friend. The other man didn't need to know exactly how closely he would be watching Anthony.

The timid blond flashed him a nervous smile. "Umm. I guess I'll have that drink then."

Silver tried to look harmless, which

wasn't easy for a strong pack alpha. What did you say to a man who smelled so divine you wanted to pounce?

Gently he guided his future mate to a table set on a dais apart from the dance floor. Currently empty, the table was reserved for him and his pack mates. It was high above the others so you could see what was going on around the club. Silver often used it as a lookout point when he was making sure no one was causing trouble.

He pulled out a chair for Anthony before seating himself to Anthony's left.

"So sweet, who is the tattoo for?"

Caramel eyes blinked rapidly. "My lover, Andrew. He died three years ago; I was with him for two."

Unable to resist the urge to comfort the smaller man, Silver stroked a hand down his arm. He was so fucking sweet the alpha wanted to gobble him up, in the best way possible, but the thought of scaring him off kept his wolf at bay despite the fact both halves of him wanted the other man with an unprecedented level of desire.

Luring a mate was a tricky business.

"Did you really come here to find a new lover?" Silver was careful to make his voice inquiring not accusing. He wanted Anthony to confide in him but he didn't want to appear pushy.

"I came here to support my friend, and I wanted to sort of shop around." Anthony blinked moisture out of his beautiful eyes, wringing Silver's heart in the process. "I'm so tired of being alone, and Steve thinks I should get out more."

"I'm sorry you lost your lover." He wasn't really sorry, but the sweet boy was obviously upset. Usually it was important to appear strong and unfazed, as wolves would attack the weakest of the pack, but he wanted to let this young man know he felt for his pain. Not sympathetic enough to want Anthony's lover back in the picture, but sympathetic nevertheless.

The sweet man nodded as he gulped back tears with obvious effort. "It's been three years. Steve's right I need to move on."

"He sounds like a good friend."

Anthony nodded. "He saved me after Drew died. I really wanted to go with him."

Silver gave Anthony's hand a gentle squeeze. "I'm very glad you didn't."

The younger man gave him a tremulous smile. "Me too."

Silver didn't waste any time. With one smooth movement he wrapped his arm around Anthony, pulling the other man closer.

Surprised, the blond almost tumbled off his seat.

"Careful, baby. I just want to get a feel for you."

Anthony glanced down. "Yes, I can see that."

Silver laughed; a loud, booming sound that carried over the club and attracted the attention of one of his pack.

Farro, a slim man with auburn hair and third in pack hierarchy, approached them. His eyes held a teasing light as he looked at them. "Hello Silver, who's your friend?"

"Farro, this is Anthony who is getting over the loss of his lover. Anthony this is Farro, one of my oldest friends." He only told his friend of Anthony's distress so that he would know Silver wasn't the source of the younger man's tears. He didn't want word getting around that he'd made the sweet man cry. The pack was filled with merciless teasers, and even their alpha wasn't completely off limits.

The light in Farro's eyes dimmed and compassion filled his eyes. The werewolf had also lost a family member in the past year. "I'm sorry to hear that, Tony. How long ago did he die?"

"Three years." Although they didn't fall, Silver could still hear the tears in his voice.

Farro gave the human a sympathetic smile, but when Anthony turned his head the wolf flashed a wicked grin at his alpha. "If you're looking for a new lover I'd be happy to vet them for you. I know most of the people at this club." Farro stepped forward and stroked Tony's hair in a soothing gesture.

A low growl vibrated Silver's chest as someone else touched what was his.

The other wolf paled and, giving a hasty bow with a submissive tilt of his head, he hastily added, "On the other hand, Silver can watch over you. He's very protective of his friends." With a quick smile and an apologetic look at his alpha, the man hurried on his way.

Smart man.

There was teasing and then there was getting your throat ripped out by a rabid alpha. Silver took the extra effort to hide his feral grin when the sweet boy looked his way.

"He was certainly in a hurry."

Silver shrugged his shoulders. "Maybe he remembered something he had to do."

He dipped into the other man's mind,

pleased when he found that despite Anthony's puzzlement at Farro's behavior he didn't regret the man leaving. Only alphas could read minds, and it was times like this that he enjoyed what a handy talent it was.

Caramel eyes blinked up at him as if sensing the intrusion.

"Let me order you a drink, sweetness. I promise to mostly behave."

Anthony's mouth twitched with the beginnings of a smile.

Silver made it his goal of the evening to see that smile in its full glory.

"Mostly?"

"Well, I can't promise the impossible." He let his eyes rake over all that exposed skin. "After all, there is only so much temptation a man should be asked to resist."

Wow, dimples.

Silver basked in the glory of Anthony's beautiful smile, his body going hard at the sight. He closed his mouth quickly before his fangs could poke through. Passion sometimes brought out his mating fangs and he didn't want to scare off the sweet, sweet man who would soon be his. Oddly enough, the more time he spent with him, the less plain the younger man looked.

"Evening sir, may I get you something?"

A young man dressed in the club colors of red and black approached.

"Evening, Kevin," Silver greeted his employee with a flicker of a glance before focusing back on Anthony. "I would like a shot of whiskey. What would you like, baby?"

"Two tequila shots with lime and salt, please," Anthony said to the waiter, flashing another dimpled smile. Silver resisted the urge to growl. Dimpled smiles should be exclusively his.

"Make that one shot and a beer," he countermanded. "I don't want you drunk."

Anthony glared, his amazing eyes sparkling in the light. "You aren't my boss to tell me what to do."

Kevin discreetly left while they argued.

Silver gripped Anthony's chin in a gentle but firm hold. "But I will be. It's important we start as we plan to continue."

Jerking his chin out of Silver's grip, he said in a deceptively quiet voice, "Who says *we'll* continue anything?"

"Call it a hunch." He slid his hands into the human's hair, jerking him close. Without giving Anthony a chance to object he took the other man's mouth in a gentle invasion.

* * * *

A rough mashing of lips Anthony could have resisted, but not the tender brushing of skin against skin, sweet and coaxing beneath his tongue. Heat whipped through his body, like an inferno as he burned with need for the gorgeous man. When Silver pulled him closer, pressing his naked chest against the other man's mesh shirt, he let a low moan rip through him.

Need filled him. With Drew the passion was flash hot, not this gentle yearning that clawed at him with the sharp talons of hunger as if his body would die if deprived of this one man's touch. When Silver lifted his mouth, Anthony followed, determined to get more of those lips flavored like paradise.

Hard hands held him back.

"Please," he whimpered in a broken voice he barely recognized as his own.

Silver's lips brushed across his, eliciting another soft sound. "Take it easy baby. You can have all the kisses you want," the deep, velvety voice promised. "Just say you'll be mine."

What? Anthony snapped back to reality. What was he doing? Almost having sex with a complete stranger seconds after meeting? He wasn't ready to belong to anyone anytime soon.

It might have been a while since Drew died but he remembered the process being slower, more meaningful. A careful dance to see if two people would mesh in and out of bed. Silver's strange grey eyes held his captive.

"You want to belong to me. I know it," he said, his voice mesmerizing in its conviction.

"Your drinks." The cheerful tone of the server broke the trance he was falling into.

What the fuck was that all about?

Anthony spared the server a smile. "Thank you." He licked his skin, salted it, licked the salt, took the shot, and bit into the lime. The combination of flavors went to his head in a fine buzz as he slowly sipped the classy imported beer. "I'll take another shot," he told the waiter who was watching him with a wide smile.

"No, he won't," Silver countermanded once again. "Go serve someone else."

The waiter abandoned them without a backward glance.

Anthony almost objected, but the look in the other man's eyes held him back.

"You've been too long without a master my sweet. You keep trying to think for yourself."

"Who said I needed a master. I'm not some silly little sub who wandered in off the streets looking for someone to take care of me," he challenged. He wasn't going to give up control to this total stranger without a few answers. Silver may be the hottest thing in the club but Anthony was a more cautious soul. Unfortunately, that caution vanished before molten silver eyes and the set of hot muscled abs he could see traced lovingly by the large man's shirt. He wondered if the hot werewolf was big everywhere; from the bulge in his pants, he thought it was a foregone conclusion. His mouth watered at the thought of finding out firsthand. Nerves thrummed through his system as he tried to decide if he was willing to give up his freedom for the chance to find out. He had a feeling that once he gave in to the gorgeous man's demands he would lose his independence forever.

"I can tell you need someone to take charge by the look in your eyes." Silver leaned forward and took Anthony's lips in a commanding kiss that demanded everything and gave even more. Fire licked down his spine as need burned in him like a bonfire.

He pulled back, reluctantly removing himself with a gentle tug from Silver's tight grip.

"I might like a man to control me, but

I'm not looking for something long term. Drew was my soul mate and I don't think I'm ready for a replacement.

Silver's handsome face drew tight. "I would never try to, my sweet. No one can replace someone once they're in your heart." One large hand pressed across Anthony's chest. "But I would be honored if you would consider placing me beside him. We don't know each other yet, but I would be happy to be your first dip into the dating pool."

Anthony snorted, trying not to choke on his beer. "I can't believe you said that with a straight face."

"Too sappy?" Silver's eyes lit with laughter.

"Yes.

Looking at the other man's handsome, stern face, Anthony wondered if he could stand to put himself in the care of a Master again. Since Drew, he hadn't trusted anyone enough to give up control. Despite what Steven might think, he didn't abstain from sex he just settled for anonymous trysts and one night stands. Letting someone close took more nerve and courage than he had before tonight. For the first time in a long while, he was tempted.

"Can you give me what I need?" They

both knew he meant more than sex. He wasn't stupid, he knew he could sex from anyone. What he really needed was someone who could support and guide him. Anthony didn't need someone to tell him what to do every second of his day. He needed someone to make it safe for him to give up control and know he would be taken care of. Someone he could trust.

There was no hesitation in the other man's answer. "Absolutely. Will you give me the chance?"

Here it was; the decision. He could toss it all away now and go back to his successful but empty life yearning for something just out of reach or he could take a chance on the gorgeous man beside him. "Okay." If his voice trembled a little in the end they both pretended not to notice.

As if worried he would take his agreement back, Silver grabbed him by the wrist, pulled him out of his chair, dragged him through the dance floor, across the lobby, and up a short set of stairs in the back hall. Thoughts of sitting and getting to know the handsome man better were subdued beneath the rush of being dragged away by a passionate stranger.

He got vague impressions of cream-colored walls and fine wood before he was rushed through a doorway and sent airborne. He landed with a gasp on a decadent pile of fluffy and silky coverings. Anthony sank into the soft bed further when a hard body covered him from chest to toe. The contrast between the two sensations revived any of the excitement lost during transit.

"I thought we were going to get to know each other first," he said once he gathered his scattered thoughts enough to form a sentence.

Silver gave him a wicked smile and a smoldering kiss. "Oh, we'll get to know each other very well soon," he promised. He slid to his feet at the bottom of the bed and, with gentle hands, removed Anthony's shoes, socks and, with a rougher touch, his pants.

He imagined he looked like he felt; a man about to be ravaged.

"I think the best way to decide if we're compatible is to do a taste test," his lover murmured.

Before he could object, Silver's mouth swooped down and swallowed his cock in one smooth motion, forcing all thoughts from his brain. He became a creature of pure sensation as wave after wave of desire rocked him to the core. Just as he was certain to shoot, the evil man lifted his mouth.

"Nooo," Anthony cried, frustrated tears filling his eyes.

"Not yet, baby. Not until I tell you." Silver's hands stroked his thighs, bringing him down from the edge.

"I changed my mind."

Silver froze.

"I just want someone to fuck me. I don't need a master."

His dark-haired nemesis chuckled. "Don't worry baby, I'll fuck you. But you're mistaken; you most definitely need a master. And I'm it."

"Sure of yourself are you?" he taunted from the comfort of the bed.

"Most definitely."

The lust in Silver's eyes made him so hard he was certain he could pound nails with his cock.

"Don't worry baby, I'll never ask you to risk this beauty on some nails," Silver's right hand slid up and down Anthony's erection, sending warning tingles up his spine.

Fuck, the man could read minds. Anthony's body thrummed with the contact, making it difficult to form complete thoughts. Touch starved. That's what he was, but his body remembered the joy of another against his. The sensation was too much.

"I'm going to come," he warned.

"No you won't." Silver's hard voice demanded obedience.

Miraculously, the burning urgency dampened to a slow fire instead of the incessant need riding his spine.

By his voice alone, Silver controlled him.

What a man.

"That's it baby," the werewolf crooned. His cock was released as Silver stood over him, slowly pulling off his shirt, exposing a lightly furred, olive-skinned chest with ripped muscles, probably from running as a wolf. All the shifters he'd ever seen were fit like Silver. Hunger for the handsome man flared like an inferno in his stomach.

When his large lover lowered his zipper, Anthony barely resisted the urge to lunge. He wanted to attack the other man with a ferocity that surprised him.

A low chuckle filled the air as Silver walked closer before stripping completely out of his remaining clothes. "Eager are you?"

"Yes, so fuck me."

"You forget who's in charge here, my sweet."

"Not me?" Anthony asked, blinking innocently.

Silver's mouth quirked in a half smile, flashing his white teeth in the dim light. "Not you." He slid one finger across Anthony's skin from shoulder to stomach, distracting him from his thoughts.

Anthony sucked in his breath as goose bumps rose along the finger's path. Need ate at him like a hungry beast. "Please fuck me," he pleaded.

Silver quirked one dark brow. "You think you're worthy of my dick?"

"No, but fuck me anyway."

"Oh I will my sweet, but later we're going to have a session that involves your fine ass and the heat of my hand."

"Sounds like a deal." Anthony gave Silver a look from beneath his lashes, a coy expression that used to bring Drew to his knees. It would probably be more effective without the suppression spell. For the first time he regretted casting it.

* * * *

Silver looked down at the feast lying on his bed and almost prematurely ejaculated for the first time in his life. Never had a man looked so damn good.

He could tell Anthony was going to blow as soon as he entered, but hell, there was no way he could make the kid wait any longer. As much as he loved to exquisitely torture his bed partners, Silver wasn't into denying himself. They would have time later to draw out their pleasure, but first he needed to take the edge off.

"I changed my mind. I'll make it up to you later, baby, but this one's going to be quick."

Even though he knew he didn't need one, he slipped on a condom so as not to worry his sweet mate. Silver didn't want their first time to cause any shadows in those beautiful caramel eyes. Later, when Anthony knew for certain what he was, they could go without.

Lubing up two fingers, Silver plunged them into the sleek, elegant body grinding beneath him.

"Ahhhh," Anthony screamed, instinctively lifting his legs so his lover could get better access.

Found it.

Silver grinned knowing his expression was probably more wolf-wicked than reassuring. He brushed against the same spot again, watching with satisfaction when the smaller man let out another yell.

"Harder."

"My pace, sweet. My pace." Removing his fingers Silver replaced them with his cock, slowly pushing his way into the hot willing body beneath him.

Gasping, Anthony flashed a taunting smile of his own. "Don't be shy, baby. Come on in."

Silver pushed all the way into the hot, silky body until he was balls deep. "I'm. Not. Shy." With each pump of his body he slammed against Anthony's prostrate, making him scream. "I just like to be certain of my welcome.

His mate's slim form bucked beneath his body, the friction amazing.

"Come," Silver whispered as he continued to nail the man's prostate over and over.

Instantly obedient, Anthony exploded. Cream burst from him in great, body shaking spurts. A moment later Silver gave a cry and collapsed on top of him before quickly moving to the side, unwilling to harm his young lover.

He wrapped himself around his smaller mate, nuzzling the fine hairs on the back of Anthony's head. "Mate," he whispered before falling asleep.

* * * *

Mate. Panic raced through Anthony's mind. Maybe he'd heard wrong. Hopefully he'd heard wrong. Every nerve in his body screamed at him to flee.

Silver was too intense.

He wasn't ready for another relationship. Excuses for leaving ricocheted like bullets across his mind.

Wiggling, he tried once again to free himself of his bigger, stronger, bedmate but Silver's hold tightened and he dragged Anthony closer until he was half lying beneath the larger man.

"Sleep, sweetness," Silver mumbled in a sleep-roughened voice.

There was no way he was going to escape before morning.

With a sigh, Anthony settled into the warm cocoon created by the werewolf, letting the comfort of heat and good sex relax him into sleep.

He could worry about the implications tomorrow.

CHAPTER THREE

Anthony woke when a stream of sunlight heated his cheek. The empty, rumpled sheets told him his bed partner was missing, and the bedside clock revealed it was still early enough he wasn't running late.

Blinking wearily he slid out of bed and picked up his pants from the night before. Memories of Silver whispering 'mate' caused shivers, only partly brought on by the coolness of the air against his shirtless skin. He doubted the possessive wolf would let him sashay out of there without a goodbye or two.

After a quick sniff, Anthony decided a shower was called for. He might have to leave wearing yesterday's pants but he didn't have to smell like sex, especially if he ran into other werekin. He wondered how Steven fared the night before. He hoped his friend had found someone to spend the night with. When Silver had dragged him from the club the last thing on his mind was his friend. He felt a pang of guilt over the desertion even as he knew Steven wouldn't mind a bit. If he was getting sex then his friend would be happy for him.

A fast shower and a stolen shirt later, Anthony left the room in search of Silver. He might not be completely sure of this mating thing, but it was impolite to leave without saying goodbye. His folks raised him better than that.

Was that bacon he smelled?

Hunger lured him down the stairs and toward the sounds of people talking.

* * * *

Silver knew the moment his lover entered the room. Inhaling deeply he wallowed in the combined smell of his delicious mate and spicy soap, an addictive combination.

"I hope you don't mind, I borrowed your shower and a shirt." Anthony's smooth tenor flowed across him, spiking his hormones like a triple shot of caffeine. He resisted the urge to turn around, throw his lover onto the table, and fuck him good morning. The only reason he wasn't still in bed with his mate was an early morning problem with a distributor. The man was lucky he didn't have his throat ripped out when he tried to get more money out of Thomas.

"Hell, if Silver minds, you can borrow my shirt," Thomas piped up from the seat opposite Silver.

Anthony was behind him, but Thomas smelled of hot need and his voice was rough with desire.

Fucker.

"He has my shirt," growled Silver, his possessiveness coming forward. If anyone was going to provide for his mate, it was him. "Come sit beside me, baby, and have some breakfast."

Need scented the air.

It took the alpha a moment to realize it poured off of all ten of the pack members sitting around the table, male and female, as they stared at the man behind him. "Stop staring," he snapped.

Instantly obedient, the pack members looked to one side, no longer looking directly behind him. "But he's sooo beautiful," Shara said in a dreamy voice.

Silver snorted and pulled out the chair beside him. "I don't think they've all had their coffee yet, my sweet. Have a seat. Shara, get my mate some breakfast."

The blonde jumped up and quickly assembled a plate brimming with more food than a werekin could eat after a full moon hunt.

"Thank you," Anthony said, his sweet voice running down Silver's spine and settling in his balls.

The flash of gold drew Silver's attention to the man beside him. He choked on his toast.

"Hey darlin', you all right." A firm pat on the back helped move his bite of bread along.

"Who are you?"

The sunburst eyes narrowed. "Sorry if my appearance isn't as appealing in the morning light."

He started to rise but Silver stopped him with a hand on his wrist. "I didn't mean that. Why are you so…" He couldn't finish under the glare of those beautiful eyes.

He thought for a moment Anthony was going to jerk out of his hands, then a flash of knowledge glowed in his remarkable eyes.

"It was a suppression spell." His mate's cheeks blushed red. "I gave myself a glamour so I wouldn't outshine Steven."

A glamour? That meant…

Thomas beat him to it. "Holy shit! This is what he really looks like?"

Silver felt everything in him tense. He looked at Anthony one more time to confirm the horrible truth; his new mate wasn't just a pretty boy, he was an obscenely beautiful man. Never in three hundred years had he ever seen anyone, male or female, more beautiful.

He was totally fucked.

Thomas started laughing like a loon.

Silver wanted to kill something, preferably his lieutenant.

"Is there a problem? I'm sorry if you felt I misled you. I didn't do it intentionally. I didn't really think I'd be with anyone the next morning."

Anthony's sweet face turned to his and Silver gave in to the need to kiss him good morning. Plunging his hand into the silky gold of his mate's hair, he controlled the depth of the kiss with a masterful touch. Slowly he parted from the man, forcing his reluctant fingers to release him. "No baby. It just means you're a little more than I was expecting. Since you can cast a glamour, does that mean you have wizard blood in you?"

Anthony nodded his head, sending a cold feeling to the bottom of Silver's stomach. Wizards notoriously hated other supernaturals.

"Forest witch on my mother's side."

Everything fell into place in Silver's mind; the rich forest smell, the golden gleaming skin and hair, and the brilliant eyes. He relaxed a bit. Forest witches have always bonded well with werekin. Maybe it would work out fine after all.

Just as he was going ask what Anthony's father was, Parker, the newest member of the pack, sauntered in. Dark-haired, with six feet of lean muscle and attitude, the young wolf swaggered into the room only to stop in the doorway. His usual cocky expression changed to bliss. "What is that amazing smell?"

Silver could pinpoint the moment the younger wolf spotted his mate. Parker's entire body seized up as he looked Anthony up and down like he was a deer the wolf was about to cull from the herd.

"Who are you?" Parker walked across the room and dipped his nose into Anthony's neck, inhaling his scent.

His mate giggled.

Silver growled, baring fangs. "Get your fucking hands off my mate before I rip them off and beat you with them."

Parker jerked back, losing his confidence beneath his alpha's gaze. "S-sorry. He just smells so good." The werewolf's nostrils flared as he started to instinctively lean towards Anthony.

Silver's hand whipped out, grabbing the other werewolf by the neck. "Don't make me repeat myself, whelp. Touch my mate again and I'll snap your fucking neck."

"Whoa. Easy, baby." Anthony's gentle voice floated across Silver's skin, easing the fury to a manageable roar. "He didn't mean anything, he's just a curious pup."

His mate's hands slid across his back in long, soothing strokes. "Let him go baby. I need to eat my breakfast before I leave, and I'm starving."

Silver shoved Parker away, watching dispassionately as the younger wolf fell to the ground. Nothing fired a wolf's instincts more than the need to protect his mate. Giving Parker one last glare as the other were rubbed his neck, he slid his fingers beneath Anthony's hair and pulled the smaller man forward to claim his lips in another kiss. Unlike the hot passionate kisses from the other night, this one was purely an act of possession. He made sure he swiped his tongue across his mate's mouth, growling a little at the amazing flavor exploding across his taste buds.

Anthony broke away first, earning a tightening grip from the alpha.

"You don't back away from me."

To Silver's surprise the smaller man's eyes flared bright gold. "I might like to be controlled inside the bedroom, but I'm in charge of my own life." He held up his hand at the sound of protest bubbling from the alpha's throat. "I don't know about this mate thing. I just wanted a one night stand to help get over Drew."

"Trust me, we're mates." Silver couldn't let the challenge stand. Especially with Parker waiting there, poised to lure his new love away. It was against the rules to force someone to be your mate; however, nothing prevented strong-armed persuasion.

He slid his arms around Anthony letting the other man feel the heat of his body. "Do you want me to be alone for the rest of my life?"

Anthony gasped. "You only get one mate?"

Silver nodded. Sliding his cheek across the human, he spread his scent across the younger man, marking him to let other werekin know this beautiful boy was taken. "I don't want to lose you, baby. What do I need to say?"

He heard Parker snort behind him.

Anthony's hands came up to stroke his head, the touch tentative, but affectionate. "I don't want you to be alone. I… I know what it's like to be alone and I wouldn't wish it on anyone."

Sweet, sweet boy. Silver almost felt bad for his manipulation.

Almost.

He stood still, letting his mate pet him.

"We'll work something out," Anthony said.

Damn right.

Silver hid his smug expression in the nape of his mate's neck, nuzzling gently. "I didn't mean to scare you."

"I was just surprised. I..." He felt Anthony swallow against his cheek. "I didn't expect to be someone's mate."

* * * *

Anthony's phone rang, his assistant's ring tone loud in the silent room. With one last pat he slid out of the werewolf's arms and pulled his phone from his pants pocket.

Ten wolves watched the movement with feral anticipation. He tried not to let it unnerve him.

"Hey, Poppet," he said into the receiver. A childhood friend since the age of six, Ellen was one of the few people he trusted to watch his back in the business world. With the fierce competition of building design he needed people he could depend on.

"Hello, sir," came Ellen's perky reply. It

was a bit of a contest between them of how quirky his pet names became and how formally she countered them.

"Those men are here for your morning meeting about the property on Sanders street."

Anthony cursed softly, earning a growl from the large were beside him. "Stall them, sweetheart. Give me twenty minutes. I'll drive over and get ready quickly."

"Hmmm. Must've been a good night." Ellen purred into the phone. "Still aren't dressed and I know you're not in your room. Congratulations on getting laid. You could just teleport over, you know."

He could feel the heat in his cheeks, but he kept his tone level. "I don't think they're ready for that. I'll see you in a little bit. Stall for me." He hung up trusting she would take care of everything until he showed.

The fact that his father was half god, half fae was not something you dumped on a new love interest. Anthony's magical heritage had been the one point of contention between him and Drew. His parents popping in and out of his life was another. And 'popping in' was not used figuratively.

A large hand reached out and gripped him firmly at the back the neck. "Is there anything you want to tell me, *mate?*" Silver's low growl raised the fine hairs across Anthony's body.

He stroked the werewolf's arm, taking away his aggression with one gentle touch. "I have to get to work. I forgot about a meeting." It was best to avoid any further discussions when he had to race to the office. He knew any discussion about his heritage would be long, involved, and frustrating.

Still gripping his nape, the large man devoured his lips in a powerful kiss. "I'll see you tonight," the alpha said. It wasn't a question.

Silver released him, allowing Anthony the freedom to nod in agreement.

"What is it you do?" Parker asked.

He was about to answer when one of the other wolves piped up. "You're Anthony Carrow," Shara said, her voice rising with excitement. "I saw your picture in one of those glossy architectural magazines, I forget which one. You designed that new hotel downtown didn't you?"

Anthony nodded. "I was the chief architect. It was one of my favorite projects." He didn't mention he was also the owner of the architectural firm. He had amassed a large fortune and now spent the time indulging in pet projects. Mostly he used his time mentoring younger architects but occasionally he got to design a building on his own. The hotel was his latest work.

Silver flashed him a brilliant smile. "Smart and beautiful."

"I've gotta go. I'm already late for a meeting. I'm hoping to buy some land for a boutique hotel I've been planning."

Silver gave his cheek a kiss. "Bye, *mate*."

Anthony wasn't sure if the emphasis was for him, or the other wolves in the room, so he just smiled and left as if the hounds of hell were on his heels. For all he knew they were.

* * * *

Silver watched his lover walk out the door, satisfied he would see the man later.

"I thought you didn't like pretty boys," Thomas said, raising an eyebrow.

"My boy isn't pretty," Silver smiled smugly, "He's beautiful." He stopped smiling as he remembered the panicked look in Anthony's eyes. If he saw the other man that evening he would be surprised. His gorgeous mate looked ready to run.

That was all right. Silver liked hunting things down.

CHAPTER FOUR

Anthony rushed to the back entrance of the building, taking the private elevator to his penthouse suite. The building was a mixed use of offices and apartments. He had a place on the top floor with the architectural offices several floors below. It wouldn't do for his employees to see him in his party clothes. They talked about him enough without seeing him coming into the building wearing leather pants instead of his usual designer suit.

In just a few minutes he was dressed and taking another elevator down to the meeting room. As soon as he stepped through the doorway he sensed something was wrong. The men who stood when he entered put off an uneven vibe; a vibe that told him they weren't human. There were three of them; all wearing sunglasses, all exuding danger.

Ellen handed him the file. "Thanks Peaches. Why don't you take the rest of the day off?"

"Don't you need me to take minutes for this meeting?"

"I think we'll be all right. This is just going to be an informal chat to get the ball rolling. Go on now, go spend some time with your family." Giving him a strange look she let him escort her to the door and close it behind her when she left. He knew there would be questions later, but for now the problem of getting Ellen to safety was solved.

"Very smooth." The tall man in the middle strode forward. "Alesandro Delora at your service." They shook hands, each sizing the other one up with a look.

Alesandro waved to the other two men. "These are my associates, Mikel and Darian."

"Nice to meet you," Anthony said, nodding to them. "Please have a seat." He slid into a chair on the opposite side of the conference table. "Is there a particular reason vampires are selling real estate?"

Alesandro looked at him, surprised. "You know about vampires?"

"Yes."

Alesandro shrugged. "We have to do something. Even though we all have investments, in this economy it is best to have other things to fall back on. Together we own a lot of property from years of acquisition. What better way to make sure we get the best return than to sell it ourselves?"

"True." Anthony dropped the questioning and opened the folder on the table.

It wasn't really his business if vampires wanted to dabble in real estate as long as they had a good deal and got the property legally to start with.

The vampires sat opposite him around the table.

"What are you, exactly?" Alesandro asked.

"What?" He looked up from his papers to see the vamps staring at him. It was reminiscent of the werewolves that morning.

Alesandro took a deep breath. "You're obviously not human. You're not werekin. I sense a bit of the fae and witch, but something else is there too."

"Nothing you need to worry about," Anthony assured him. He hated going over his genetics with strangers. It wasn't really any of their business, not to mention people rarely believed him. It was difficult to explain when you were the grandson of a god.

He got a long look before the vampire shrugged his shoulders. "Fair enough."

They were in the middle of negotiations when the door burst open and two werekin rushed in. One was dark-haired, in a leather jacket and pants, the other a dirty blond dressed in jeans and a t-shirt; both bared their fangs as they entered. Alesandro and his blood mates stood to meet this new enemy. To Anthony's surprise the vampires shoved him protectively behind the trio.

"Step away from the alpha mate," one of the werekin growled. Anthony didn't recognize the voice but he had no doubt his new lover sent them; confirming his belief that Silver was the alpha in the pack hierarchy. Not to mention the wolf last evening had bared his neck to his lover, indicating a lower rank.

"We aren't going to let you harm him." Alesandro's voice broke into his thoughts.

"I don't think they're here to hurt me." He remembered the two werekin from breakfast earlier, even though they hadn't been introduced.

"Silver sent us to protect you," the blond insisted, trying to talk around the vampires to Anthony.

"You know these two?" Alesandro looked over his shoulder to get confirmation.

"We haven't been introduced but I'm almost positive they belong to my boyfriend's pack."

"Boyfriend?"

The two wolves glared at the vampires. "I'm Callen and this is Scott. Anthony is Silver's mate," the blond said. "If you hurt him, blood will run in the streets between our clans."

"That's a pretty visual," Anthony said in a dry voice. Tired of the posturing he walked around the vampires to confront the two werekin. "As much as I appreciate you coming to my rescue," he made sure his tone indicated that he didn't appreciate it at all, "You interrupted a meeting I was having with these gentlemen."

"We were sent to protect you," the blond insisted. The werekin glared at the vampires. He didn't know if they were more frustrated he was alone with three vamps or that they didn't need to save him.

Anthony let out a put upon sigh. "As long as you don't protect me from lucrative business deals you can stay. Over there." He pointed to some seats at the far end of the table. "Sit."

"If you belong to such a powerful werewolf, where's your collar?" Alesandro asked. His sharp gaze zeroed in on Anthony's bare neck. "I can't believe he'd let you go around unmarked. You're too beautiful to wander around free."

He bristled at the vampire's remark. "You'd be surprised at how long I've been wandering around without someone to look after me."

The werekin responded as if Anthony wasn't there. "Silver will see he gets one," Callen said.

"All I wanted was a nice business meeting. Not a supernatural soap opera," Anthony grumbled. "I don't have a collar. Silver and I are still working on our relationship."

"He's newly mated," Darian offered.

Alesandro sucked in his breath. "Why is he allowed out on his own?" he demanded of the two werewolves. "Silver is the most powerful wolf in the states. His mate would be a blank check if captured." The vampire glared at the two men like they had any say in whether Anthony was kept in a collar or not.

"Because *he* is a grown man," Anthony said, sitting back down and flipping through paperwork. "Now about your property. I still think the price is a little steep, what's your final offer?"

"It's yours," Alesandro interrupted. "In exchange for better relations with the werekin."

"Is there bad relations between you?" Anthony didn't really know anything about the relationship between different paranormal communities, except for the fae where he knew more than he wanted.

"There is always a bit of discord when paranormals share territory."

"What he means is we share but don't like each other," Darian said with a growl.

"If you could put in a good word with the alpha it might help ease tensions," Alesandro agreed.

Anthony thought it over then shook his head. "No. I'll give you a fair price. My relationship with Silver is new enough I don't want to start out with him owing anyone."

Alesandro nodded. "Fair enough." His eyes lit with curiosity when he asked, "How new is your relationship?"

"It started yesterday."

"That *is* new."

Anthony shrugged. "Now if you gentlemen will be seated we can finish our negotiations."

The rest of the meeting went smoothly; the vamps were willing to go down to his price. After all, if they were willing to give it to him for free why not let him have it for whatever price he mentioned. He wasn't fooled. He knew they hoped he would put in a good word for Silver despite what he'd said. Anthony didn't take it personally; it was good business. Because on the other end, if they screwed him over the wolves would report back to Silver and they'd get in trouble anyway.

He shook the vampire's hand as they sealed the deal. Satisfied with their transaction, Anthony decided to mention an idea he had. Alessandro seemed likeable for a vampire; polite, calm, and didn't let a little thing like growling pack mates bother him. You had to admire a man who could negotiate under pressure.

"I was wondering if you'd be interested in a proposition," he said leaning back in his chair.

"What kind of proposition," the vampire asked, mirroring Anthony's casual stance.

"I'm looking for a vampire consultant."

"What would I be consulting on?" Alesandro leaned forward, his expression cool but interested.

"My new hotel, the one I'm building on your old property, is going to be a paranormals only hotel. I'd like to have specialized rooms for different types of paras. I obviously have werekin I can ask about their accommodation preferences, but no vamps. Would you be interested in being on my board?"

"What would I have to do?"

Anthony shrugged. "Answer my questions when I call, draft a preliminary list of vampire needs so I can design rooms accordingly, and be available to give me feedback. Almost all of which can be done remotely."

"I'll do it," Alesandro announced. "With the caveat that I can always stay at the hotel free of charge."

Anthony smiled, "You have yourself a deal."

The men shook on it, ignoring the werewolves growling at the contact.

CHAPTER FIVE

The ringing of the telephone woke Anthony from a deep sleep. The past few weeks he'd been staying late at the office trying to finalize plans for his hotel. Stumbling to bed in the early hours didn't make him happy to hear his phone ringing before noon.

Steven's too cheerful voice yelled in his ear. "Wakey, wakey, pretty man."

"Someone had best be dying," Anthony growled. He hated, positively hated, waking up, especially when he was dreaming of hot sex with a certain dark-haired wolf.

Steven laughed across the line. "Not yet, but Silver threatened me if I don't have you there tonight."

It had been exactly one week since his run-in with the gorgeous alpha wolf. A week of hot dreams where they fucked like bunnies before sleeping entwined like long-time lovers. He woke each morning with spunk on his chest, panting like he'd finished a marathon of sex. He'd only seen the werewolf two other times because of scheduling and, frankly, he was scared. It was one thing to enjoy some hot dominant loving, but with Silver he was certain the man could become his whole world. After losing Drew he didn't think he could go through that again.

What if he fell in love and the alpha wolf died? Losing Drew almost killed him. He knew losing Silver would finish the job. Although they were harder to kill than a regular human, werekin weren't bulletproof.

"I don't know, Steven," he stalled.

"I can't believe you have the hottest guy in town panting after you and you have to think about it." There was a bite to Steven's voice, reminding Anthony his friend was still looking for his mate. For the first time he wondered if the other wolf had his eye on the alpha.

"Did I interrupt your plans?" he asked cautiously. "Did you have your sights on him?" Steven was his closest friend. He would never take someone his best friend had designs on but he didn't think Silver would take a substitute now. The alpha was fixated on him, and was even interested before he saw beneath the disguise. That was the one thing Anthony clung to. Silver wanted him before he knew what Anthony really looked like. His looks had always been a barrier in the past where men only wanted something pretty on their arm, not someone who could think for himself. Anthony might like to be overpowered in the bedroom but he wasn't a brainless puppet waiting for someone to tell him to wipe his butt.

Steven's voice pulled him back into the conversation. "Honey, everyone has their sights on him. You were just lucky enough to be the one he wants."

"I just can't, Steven." He couldn't explain to his best friend how much he wanted to be Silver's mate, but fear held him back. Loss was not something he could go through again.

"What did that fucker do to you Tony?" Steven's voice hardened. "If he hurt you, alpha or not, I'll kick his ass."

Anthony smiled at his friend's protective tone. Despite knowing all of his secrets, Steven still thought to look out for him. "I'm scared. I can't go through losing another one."

The burst of laughter from the other end of the phone was the final straw after a week of long work hours, worrying over a new relationship, and reliving the loss of his previous lover over and over in his mind.

"Fuck you," Anthony shouted, slamming down the phone.

The phone rang a minute later.

He was an idiot for answering but he did it anyway; Steven was too good a friend to ignore. Besides, the bastard would just show up at his doorstep if he didn't answer the phone.

"I wasn't laughing at you."

"It felt like it," he sulked, not so eager to forgive and forget.

"Werekin are very difficult to kill. Fuck, I don't even think we can get sick. Have you ever known me to be ill?"

"No." Anthony had to admit, Steven was never sick a day in his life, of course he wasn't either, but that was for different reasons. "But you could get shot or something."

It was a weak argument but it was all he could think of. He couldn't make his lover bulletproof and it wasn't unusual for hunters to try to take them out.

A long sigh came over the phone. "Stop making excuses and go talk to Silver. He'll be able to help you with your fears."

"Fine, but don't laugh at me again or I'll set your ass on fire."

"Yes, sir." Steven's tone was amused, but they both knew he could do it. Only half of his blood was forest witch, the rest was far more dangerous.

* * * *

In the privacy of his office Silver paced

back and forth. He didn't want anyone else to see his nerves. He'd never live it down if his pack saw he was a jumbled mess over one little human, or not-so-human. Curiosity about his lover's genetics bubbled up, causing Silver to start wondering what his lover could do with his abilities. Anthony was surprisingly quiet about his powers. Silver wasn't worried; his mate would tell him everything when he was ready.

If Steven did his job his mate would return tonight. Silver might be unwilling to pressure his mate, but he had no ethical problems forcing Anthony's friend to do the work for him. He gave Steven an ultimatum. Either produce his mate or have his membership revoked. When it came to getting his mate, Silver had no problems being a bastard.

"He's here Silver," Farro said from the doorway. "And he's loaded for bear. You'd best get down there before someone poaches your boy."

Farro jumped to one side as Silver stormed out the door. "Anyone who poaches my boy won't live to regret it," he growled. How dare they think to touch what was his. A small voice in the back of his mind reminded him that he had yet to place a collar around his lover. That was something he was going to fix right now. No one was going to think his man was available a moment longer. He wondered if there was any way he could get Anthony to always wear a disguise. Not that it would fool a werekin, but it might help them look elsewhere if he didn't walk around looking like every gay man's wet dream. Hell, he could probably convert some straight guys.

Determined to rescue his mate Silver marched through the hall, bursting into the club. Scanning the crowds, his heart skipped a beat when he saw his beautiful man surrounded by the biggest predators in the club. Only two of the group were human.

Anthony stood sleek and beautiful in a silver mesh shirt and tight black leather pants. Silver bemoaned the covering of that fine chest with its sweet nipples while feeling a flash of possessive pleasure that the others didn't get to view all that glorious golden skin. Without the suppression spell, Anthony's skin took on a glittery hue, making him wonder if all of his mate's magical abilities came from his witch mother. He made a mental note to ask the beauty for more information about his paternal line.

Silver leapt to the dance floor, blithely shoving away a vampire who had an arm wrapped around his baby.

"Hey, man," the vampire said, but when turned and saw it was Silver he slunk away.

Anthony looked up and Silver fell into the adoring look in the other man's gaze. Damn he was stunning.

"I missed you, baby," he admitted before taking Anthony's mouth in a possessive kiss, staking his claim to any who cared to look. Everyone there would know this man was taken, even if he had to have it tattooed on Anthony's forehead. Hmmm, he wondered if he could get away with that.

When he finally lifted his mouth, he was pleased by the dazed expression in his mate's caramel eyes. "Did you miss me?" he asked in a low purr.

"Y-yeah." Anthony stammered. His eyes were unfocused, his pupils blown with lust, and his lush mouth swollen from Silver's kiss. He'd never seen the man look better.

He couldn't stop the pleased smile on his face. He had reduced his baby to a stutter. He felt like a god.

"So, Silver, you going to share your new find?" He turned to face the speaker. Aslic, a vampire he'd shared many a bottom boy with in the past, was watching Anthony with a hungry expression in his icy blue eyes. If he was fair he couldn't blame the vamp. It wasn't as if they didn't have a history, but this was his man and Silver barely checked his wolf from taking over and ripping out the man's throat. Only centuries of being friends saved the vamp's life. Leaning forward he whispered into the Aslic's ear. "If you ever touch my boy I will rip out your heart and eat it for breakfast."

The words were a solemn vow, and from the flash of fear in Aslic's eyes he knew it. Satisfied the vampire would spread the word Silver wrapped an arm around his boy and led him from the room.

"One of these days we should actually dance at your dance club," Anthony teased, following Silver's lead with a smooth, slinky step that inflamed his lust and made his wolf lunge at the reins.

"I'm so glad you came back, baby." He couldn't put into words the fear he'd had that his beautiful boy would never return. "Let's go to my room so we can talk."

Anthony gave a dirty chuckle that shouldn't be able to come out of such a sweet looking mouth. "Yeah, let's go and *talk*."

* * * *

Anthony waited to speak until they entered the privacy of Silver's room.

"It wasn't you, love. It was me," he gave a broken laugh. "I've become a cliché. I can't stand the thought of losing someone else I love."

Silver looked at him, stunned. "You love me?"

Anthony felt the blush burn his cheeks. Shit. Maybe he spoke too soon. He didn't know how it worked with werewolves.

He walked past Silver to sit on the bed. Once seated, he patted the spot beside him. "Come here, honey."

"Honey?" Silver gave him the quirky smile he so loved. "I don't think anyone has ever called me by a pet name before."

"No?"

Silver gave a soft chuckle. "No."

"Is it because you're Mr Alpha Wolf?"

Anthony watched with amusement as Silver's eyes went wide with surprise. "How did you find out?"

Anthony ticked the points off with his fingers. "You growl and make people jump, all the others defer to you, and the vampire I met told me you were the strongest wolf in the States. It wasn't that hard to put together.

Besides, I heard what you told Mr Smooth out there."

"Mr Smooth." Silver chuckled. "I'll have to remember that one, but you should stay away from vampires."

"I can't. I'm going into business with Alesandro."

Silver narrowed his eyes. "Alesandro, as in the leader of the vampires Alesandro? Darian told me you met with a vamp but didn't tell me which one."

Damn, he hoped he didn't get the werewolf in trouble.

"That's the one." He didn't mention he was unaware Alesandro was the vampire leader. He'd thought he was just a businessman who also happened to be a vamp.

"I won't change my business to suit you. You'll have to trust I know what I'm doing." He thought for a moment Silver was going to argue but Anthony slid to his knees, maneuvering between the alpha's feet until he pressed his body up against the man's thighs. "Do you trust me?" He looked up to meet the eyes of his lover.

Silver cupped Anthony's cheek in his large hand. "Of course I trust you. It's the rest of the world I can't trust. Would you mind if I wrapped you in bubble wrap and put you in a sealed room?"

"Yeah."

"Damn, I was afraid you'd say that." Amusement sparkled in the alpha's eyes.

From his place on the carpet, Anthony slid off Silver's left shoe and sock. "You're going to have to let me make some decisions on my own." He slid off Silver's right shoe and sock. "And I'll let you be protective as long as you're not overbearing." He looked his lover straight in the eyes. "Besides, I don't think I can live any longer without you. I dream about you at night, I think about you during the day, and I come thinking about you both of those times. If we don't do something soon, I'll never be able to concentrate again. I figure you're just the man to take care of that problem."

Silver reached down and lifted Anthony's chin. "Baby, I'll take you any way I can get you." The alpha's grey eyes met him with such serious intent, Anthony knew if he said he needed more time, this wonderful man would give it to him.

"No more hiding Silver. I'm ready to be yours."

He looked up to see a wide smile on his gorgeous mate's face that matched the welcoming light in Silver's eyes.

Strong hands lifted him to his feet.

The werewolf stayed sitting. "Will you allow me to mark you as mine?"

* * * *

"Absolutely," Anthony said with a smile. "Will you be mine also?" His beautiful boy couldn't meet his eyes when he asked. Silver knew this was important to his shy lover. Anthony was asking for exclusivity in their relationship. It wasn't uncommon for werewolves to have communal sex due to their pack nature, but the thought of another touching Anthony caused Silver's fangs to drop. There would be no sharing this one. "Yes, I'll also be completely yours. Agreed?"

He saw the relief in his beloved's eyes as Anthony nodded. "Agreed."

Gentle hands reached up to unbutton his shirt. He grabbed his mate's wrists. "I don't think so baby. Strip and then lay yourself on the bed."

He saw Anthony swallow. "Am I your mate and master, or not?" he demanded.

His mate nodded and started removing his clothing.

"Don't think this gets you out of a full pack wedding. I want to make sure everyone sees us bond." There was no doubt in Silver's mind that if he didn't make it clear to everyone they were mates someone would take it into their head to challenge him. Parker was most likely the prime candidate. "Wait there. I have something for you."

Anthony's face lit up. Oh, he could see the way to his pretty boy's heart was presents. He would have to make sure his baby got them on a regular basis. Chuckling, he walked over to the dresser, pulling a key out of his pocket as he went. He unlocked the top drawer and removed a slim bamboo box. Smiling, he brought the box back to the bed pleased to see an obedient lover lying on the bed waiting for his next command.

Silver's cock went as hard as steel. "Damn you're a beautiful man."

He watched with pleasure as Anthony crawled with sensuous grace to the end of the bed before kneeling again. Damn, if he weren't hard before, that would've done the trick.

"You have something for me?" He heard the satisfaction in Anthony's voice but he let it slide. The man had a right to be proud.

He turned the box so the clasp was facing his lover. A flick of his thumb popped the latch free. He opened the box towards Anthony, exposing a burnished gold collar encrusted with diamonds and emeralds lying on a bed of red velvet. The width of the band gave it the look of a torque from Ancient Egypt. Despite the jewels, it exuded luxurious masculinity.

"Wow." Anthony reached out with one finger, brushing lightly across the jewels as if afraid to touch it fully.

"You can hold it, baby. It's yours." Silver lifted it from its velvet bed, dropping the box gently on the carpet so he could slide the necklace around his mate's neck. Murmuring a few words he engaged the locking spell. Without the counter spell and a drop of Silver's blood the collar was impossible to remove. It would also provide Anthony with some magical protection, but he told his mate none of that. Instead he brushed back his boy's long hair and admired the glowing gold and jewels against the flawless skin.

"Perfect," he declared. It wasn't because his mate was so incredibly beautiful, but because the look in Anthony's eyes said he thought Silver was.

"I should get my hair cut," Anthony grumbled, as his fingers brushed the collar with a reverent touch.

"No. You're perfect just as you are." Silver wasn't going to be the one to tell the man that the long hair made him look like an angel. There was a limit to how romantic he could get and still keep his image as the pack badass. He helped Anthony off the bed and led him to the dresser mirror. "See."

"It's beautiful," the sleek blond said in a hushed voice. Silver noticed with amusement that Anthony didn't even look at his own reflection. His eyes were on the necklace.

"Yes, it is," he agreed, watching Anthony. He'd saved the collar for two hundred years to give it to the right man and now he'd found him. The presence of the collar would tell everyone that this was his man. To touch him would mean death or dismemberment.

Silver felt a thrill of possession as he led his mate back to bed. Anthony lay down beside him snuggling into his embrace.

"Come live with me."

He felt Anthony's body jerk beside him. "I don't know Silver." His mate's heart hammered beneath him. Fear scented the air with a sour smell.

Silver laughed, he couldn't help it. "So, my being a were doesn't even stir your pulse, but moving in with me causes a panic attack."

A flush ran up Anthony's body, Silver could almost feel the heat. Enchanting.

"I... I just think it's too soon."

Silver brushed a finger across a strip of bare flesh above the collar on Anthony's neck. "I have already chosen you, may I mark you?"

Anthony tilted back his head. "Please."

He lapped at his mate's neck, absorbing the scent and taste of the only man he would ever be with again. Fangs knifed through his gums. Unable to ignore his wolf's need to mark what was his Silver plunged his fangs into the smaller man. Wet heat, hot spice, and something that was inalienably his mate rolled across his tongue. After a few more swallows he removed his fangs from his lover's delicate skin, licking carefully at the marks and knowing that while in a few hours they would completely disappear, his scent would remain embedded in his lover for several weeks, weeks where his scent would scare off any werekin who wandered too close to his man.

"That was amazing," Anthony said, his eyes wide with rapture. "You can bite me anytime."

Silver laughed with relief. He'd learned from other werekin that not all mates appreciated a good mating bite. He was pleased that his mate wasn't one of those. "I'll keep that in mind baby. I'll keep that in mind." Now probably wasn't the time to tell his mate that he would be marked regularly to keep mate poachers away. There were a few werekin who focused on trying to lure away those who were already mated.

He hoped Anthony didn't mind having his freedom curtailed by bodyguards. There was nowhere he was going alone now, except Silver's bed.

"Now bend over my knees and present me with that gorgeous ass of yours."

Anthony gave him an anxious look beneath his lashes, so pretty.

"Come on baby. Don't make me wait. You made me wait a week before agreeing to be my mate, you deserve punishment. That collar says that I'm the only one allowed to discipline you."

In one smooth, well-practiced motion his baby lay across his lap.

"Someone is used to being spanked."

"Not for a while," Anthony gasped.

Silver smoothed a hand over his mate's sweet ass, the one he'd noticed that very first night. His palm absorbed the smooth texture of his Anthony's silky skin wrapped over a tight muscular butt. "How often do you work out, baby?"

Silver could feel his lover's cock growing hard between his legs.

"Every morning."

"Keep up the good work. This is one of the finest asses I've ever seen." And he'd seen a lot. Not that he was going to share that information with his mate. "I want you to count. I'm going to give you ten smacks and if you miss I won't fuck you." It was a baseless threat. Nothing would stop him from fucking that fine ass, but he wanted Anthony to try. This was the tamest of the things he would do to this beautiful creature as he learned his mate inside out.

He swung down his arm connecting to the pale, firm ass.

Lightning crackled around the room. He didn't know a storm was moving in.

"One," Anthony grunted.

Silver smacked his ass again. He flinched when a bolt of electricity crackled by his foot.

"Sorry."

"You want to tell me about that, baby, before I get fried?"

"I usually have better control. I told you it's been a while."

Silver flipped Anthony over until his

bare ass hit the bed. Tilting up his lover's face he saw lighting flash in his eyes.

"That's incredible." A sense of awe came over the alpha. His mate wasn't just a wood witch-fae, he was a force of nature. "Why do you do that?"

Anthony looked down at his feet. One shoulder came up in a half-hearted shrug.

"Don't lie to me or I'll turn your ass into a ball of fire."

"My grandfather is Zeus," he mumbled.

Silver laughed. Laughed until his eyes watered and he realized his lover wasn't kidding. That sobered Silver right up."Like the one and only ruler of the heavens?"

Anthony nodded.

"Shit."

"Do you still want me?"

Silver was certain he must have heard wrong. "Why wouldn't I want you?"

Anthony shrugged. "Drew always had a problem with my control issues."

"I don't have a problem with them honey. The beauty of mating with a werewolf is that I can withstand a little bolt of lightning, but I'll make sure your ass pays for each little jolt. Now back over my knee." With a quick glance at his face, Anthony lay back over his knees.

Silver scanned his lover's mind and felt his anxiety. "What are you worried about?"

"That you'll decide I'm too much trouble," he confessed.

Silver slapped him on the ass, causing his mate to yelp.

"Ouch."

"That's what you get for doubting me. Werekin don't abandon their mates just because they have problems. Your issues are a little stranger than most subs but it isn't anything I can't handle."

He was glad his mate's face was pointed away so he didn't know the huge fib Silver just told. He was certain it showed on his face. Not about keeping Anthony, nothing could stop him from claiming his mate, but about being able to handle him. How do you handle someone for who the normal rules didn't apply?

"Ten more baby, two penalty for holding back on me. We have to be completely honest with each other if we are going to make this work."

As he spanked his lover, Silver wondered how many more surprises he could handle.

Anthony counted until his pale pink ass turned a flaming red and Silver could feel proof of his mate's arousal leaking through his leather pants.

"You like this don't you baby?" Silver said, running a soothing hand over Anthony's burning hot skin. Feeling the heat of his mate's flesh beneath his fingers made him harder than stone.

Anthony nodded. Silver slid his fingers into his lover's hair pulling Anthony's head up to lick at the salty flavor of tears dripping down his cheeks. The flavors of need and his lover's underlying spiciness danced across his tongue.

"So beautiful," said Silver, his tone possessive. "So mine."

He helped his golden lover to his shaky feet. "Climb onto the bed, hands and knees. I want to fuck your cherry red ass."

* * * *

Anthony's rear was on fire. He could probably roast marshmallows with the thing, but desire and his leaking cock had him swiftly following Silver's demands. He was still amazed that the werewolf hadn't cared about his grandfather. When Drew found out it had caused one of their few fights. His previous master was a gentle man who'd loved Anthony but had hated the fact he was related to a god because it brought his own religious beliefs into question. He tried to explain there were many deities, but Drew had believed in one god and at times had hated Anthony for proving it wasn't true.

Behind him he heard the rustle of clothing removed and the sound of a lube cap popping as his shifter lover slicked himself for entry. A gentle touch pressed against his opening. "Relax, baby, take my fingers in. I don't want to hurt you."

Leaning forward on his elbows, Anthony presented his ass relaxing his muscles for Silver's entry. A soft moan sounded behind him.

"Beautiful, you are so fucking beautiful."

Two fingers, then three, then the blunt end of something larger pressed against him. With a sigh Anthony relaxed his muscles as Silver pushed inside in one smooth movement.

"Oooh." It felt so damn good.

Silver froze inside him. "Okay, baby?"

"If you would move," Anthony snapped, immediately aware of his mistake.

The cool tone of his lover enforced his error. "I think you still don't realize who's in charge here." Silver slid out, before slamming back in and nailing his gland. "I will be in charge of our pleasure and if I want to stay inside you, unmoving for eternity, I will."

"I'll be dried up corpse by then," Anthony said, tightening his grip from the inside.

Silver howled. "Sneaky bastard."

Before he could brace himself properly, his wolf lover rode him hard. Silver pumped into him like a man with something to prove. Hard, slamming strokes sent Anthony to the edge over and over until he couldn't remember the time, place, or even his name. The only thing in his world was Silver sliding inside him with his hard, hard cock. On impulse he reached to touch himself only to be slapped away.

"Mine," Silver growled nipping his neck in retaliation.

His lover wrapped a long-fingered hand around Anthony's cock, squeezing it just right. He bit his lip to hold in the shout.

"Come on, baby, give it up."

He let go, cream bursting from him like a geyser. Only Silver could make him come so much.

"Remember that. Only me," his commanding lover ordered.

He felt Silver's climax pouring into him,

binding them as one.

"Now you're mine." He heard the satisfaction in the werewolf's tone and refrained from telling Silver he was his before they'd had sex. If the man wanted to believe having sex claimed him, who was Anthony to object?

Boneless, he drifted away on a sea of sensation. Silver's touch vanished for a moment only to replaced by a warm cloth a few seconds later. Anthony's ass still burned but the feel of the cool cloth drained away some of the heat. He could've healed it himself but he didn't want Silver to think he cheated. Now wasn't the time for a showy burst of power. Now was the time to let his lover take care of him.

"Thank you," he said, sleepily.

"I will always take care of you baby," Silver wrapped his body around Anthony's.

It felt good to sleep in another man's arms again. He'd have to work something out with his schedule so he could sleep with Silver every night even though the wolf's place was further than his own cozy apartment and it would take longer to get to work. With his lover's arms around him, Anthony slipped into his first good sleep in years, comforted by the knowledge that this lover, his mate, his master, wouldn't be taken away by illness or time but be by his side forever.

The End

BAITING BEN
MOON PACK
BOOK TWO

After leaving his old pack in Alaska, Benjamin is looking for a man to call his own. Unfortunately, just as he finds Thomas, a man from his past comes to claim him. What is he going to do when two gorgeous werewolves both want him for their mate?

Baiting Ben

MOON PACK, BOOK 2

AMBER KELL

SILVER PUBLISHING
Published by Silver Publishing
Publisher of Erotic Romance

DEDICATION:

I dedicate this book to everyone who loves
wolves
and the idea of people turning into them.

CHAPTER ONE

Benjamin Sallen entered the club with wide eyes and a hopeful heart. It was a toss-up what was more fascinating; the flashing lights, the flow of dancing bodies writhing half naked across the floor, or the scantily clad waiters sashaying around with trays of food? After filling out innumerable forms to validate his werekin status, he was finally allowed through the club doors.

His enhanced werewolf senses absorbed the smells of sweat, lust, and sex. Never had he gotten so hard, so fast, but the pheromones filling the room would make anyone want to have sex. Ben had come to find a mate, but at that moment he would take hot, sweaty sex with a total stranger if it would take the edge off. As it was, his dick was trying to burst through the zipper of his favorite jeans. He wondered if this was the type of club that had a room in the back for the convenience of its members.

Ben jumped back as a wereleopard slammed his partner against the wall and started dry humping him. Maybe they didn't need a private area. Shaking his head, he walked through the dance floor, towards the bar. His throat was dry and he didn't have to work tomorrow. His job as an independent CPA let him set his own hours and prevented him from having to answer embarrassing questions about why he couldn't work on days close to a full moon.

After months of settling into his new environment and living without a pack, he yearned for the touch of another werekin. Even the brief brush of flesh from the shifters on the dance floor helped soothe the lonely animal beneath his skin. Despite leaving his Alaskan pack only six months ago, he was desperate for the company of others like him. Hunting under a full moon wasn't the same without a pack; it lacked the joyous luster, and the prey he could catch was more of the rabbit variety than a fully-grown deer.

Purchasing the club membership was his chance at a new life. If he met and mated with a local werekin he could gain acceptance into the pack. Even if he hooked up with another lone wolf, at least they could become a pack of two. In werekin culture anything was better than one. Lone creatures didn't survive long in the big bad world, especially small ones. At five feet nine inches, Ben was on the short side for a wolf shifter. He blamed that on his human mother. If he was full-blooded he would easily have topped six feet. At least he could shift. He'd heard of half-blooded werekin who were unable to shift but still felt the call of the moon. Ben decided they must be in a special type of hell, one he was lucky enough not to be a part of.

Using his smaller size to slip through the crowds, Ben made his way to the long wooden bar covering most of the back wall. The bartender moved with a fluidity that screamed cat shifter.

"What can I get you?" The bartender batted his long sable lashes over a pair of piercing sea green eyes. "Besides me."

Ben chuckled. "A rum and coke, please."

"Oooh a polite one." The bartender's hands moved so fast the motion blurred. In seconds he was presenting Ben's drink with a flourish and a flirty wink. "Anything else?"

After giving the cute cat a tip in the glass jar beside him, Ben flashed a grin of his own. "Not right now, but I'll let you know if that changes."

It wouldn't. He was looking for one of his own kind. In his wilder days the cat would've been a prime hookup, but he was looking for something more permanent. Ben wanted a mate. He wouldn't get it where he came from. At the Great Claiming none of the werekin had stepped forward to choose him. Maybe if Dillon had been home things would've been different.

Maybe.

An image of a tall, dark werewolf with forest green eyes flashed in his mind. Ben ruthlessly pushed it away along with his feelings of longing. It had hurt to leave the pack knowing he'd never see the handsome man again, but Dillon was part of his past and tonight was about securing his future.

"Hello there, cute stuff," a rough voice spoke from behind him. He turned to see a huge man with cold black eyes looking him over like Ben was a prime piece of meat he wanted to devour.

"Um. Hi." He gave a polite smile and shifted a bit to the side to look around the other man. A sniff proved the guy was werekin, but not one with any mate potential. He didn't give off the right scent.

To Ben's shock the man settled a heavy arm around him. "What do you say you and I get to know each other better? I'm Ned, what's your name?" It was more a statement than a question, as the other man was already lifting him off his barstool and guiding him towards the exit.

"B-Ben." Panic rabbited in his chest. Great, his first time in the club and already he was in trouble. Why did things like this always happen to him? All he wanted to do was meet the werewolf of his dreams and settle down, not be kidnapped by a Neanderthal.

"There you are, honey. Ned, thank you for finding him for me."

"Thomas." Ned's arm fell off his shoulders so quickly Ben lost his balance, causing him to stumble into the speaker. Firm arms wrapped around him, surrounding him in a comforting embrace. He had the oddest sensation of coming home.

"Hello, honey." Ben's quick glance up gave him an impression of laughing hazel eyes and a wide white smile before warm lips descended and kissed him to within an inch of his life. Heat burned through his body. Whimpering he moved closer to the other man, rubbing his erection against the newcomer. The man called Thomas, felt long, hard, and perfect against him. The smell of wet dew on a grassy meadow filled his senses. He fought back the urge to howl at the rightness of his scent.

His.

The stranger pulled back. Ben snarled,

his gums burning as his teeth elongated in preparation to bite. His wolf wanted to mark the other man so everyone could see. How dare he pull away, the man was his! He battled his instincts to take the larger man down like a lame deer. To bite him, fuck him, and make sure everyone knew he was claimed. Startled by the violence of his thoughts, Ben stepped back.

"I guess he *is* yours," Ned said behind him. "You better keep an eye on him before some mate hunter steals him away." The words trailed off as Ned walked back into the crowd, quickly swallowed by the crowd of dancing people.

Trying to subdue his oddly aggressive wolf, Ben gave his head a little shake. As one of the least alpha members of the pack, he was surprised at this sudden compulsion to claim the other man. Hope burst through him as he wondered if maybe he'd found what he was looking for after all.

A small part of him protested that this man wasn't Dillon. Ben ruthlessly suppressed it and turned his attention on the tall, dark man who looked like a model from a glossy magazine. The kind you had to read with one hand.

* * * *

Thomas looked down at the pretty red-haired wolf and almost came right then. Gold eyes, an aquiline nose, and lips so lush they would make a straight man dream of fucking men. He'd seen prettier men, his alpha had the most beautiful man on the planet for his partner, but he'd never met one so compelling.

Mate.

The word whispered across his mind, a message from his inner wolf. Everything fell into place, the smell, the looks, and the incredible kiss. There was no doubt in his mind that the little wolf beside him was his mate.

"My name's Benjamin," the pretty man said, holding out his hand.

"Thomas Moon." He waited for the younger man to claim his affiliation. In werekin culture your last name indicated the pack you belonged to. When Benjamin didn't answer he decided subtlety was wasted on his mate. "Where's your pack?"

A chill came into Ben's gold eyes. The smaller werewolf backed away until there was an uncomfortable foot of space between them. Thomas resisted the urge to grab Benjamin and drag him back into his arms where he belonged.

"I left my pack. I have lone wolf status."

Fear trickled up Thomas's spine like a winter chill. Lone wolves were dangerous. Most of them went solo because there was something wrong with their psyche that prevented them from traveling in a pack. Other times it was because the pack found something wrong with the werewolf and banished him. There was rarely a good reason a wolf chose to travel alone. Looking around Thomas realized they couldn't address something this important in a crowded club. They needed privacy.

"Come with me."

A wary look came into Ben's eyes. Smart man. "I just want to talk. I'll even leave the door unlocked so you can go whenever you want to," he promised. He didn't want to scare the man off, but he really wanted to talk to him in a quieter area.

After a long moment his mate nodded. "All right."

* * * *

Ben followed the handsome werewolf up a small flight of stairs. It was odd to see a pack in an urban environment. Growing up in the wilds of Alaska didn't prepare him for the strangeness of city wolves. The man walking before him looked cosmopolitan and suave, like a werewolf version of James Bond. Watching Thomas's fine ass flex as they climbed the stairs sent sparks of desire dancing up his spine.

"Stop watching my ass."

"Nope," Ben replied. "I'm enjoying the view too much. If you didn't want me staring you shouldn't be so gorgeous." He was surprised at his own daring, but pleased when Thomas turned his head briefly to flash him a smile before continuing upstairs.

A beautiful man in a jewel-encrusted collar waylaid them at the top of the steps.

"Thomas, you must tell Silver I don't need guards to watch my every step. I practically trip over them. Please, please intervene."

The stunning creature clasped Thomas's hands while he pled.

"No, Anthony, you need guards."

He felt bad for the beauty when Anthony's face took on a look of such disappointment. He felt his own heart clench in sympathy. Those sad eyes looked away and latched onto Ben. "You found your mate." With a dizzying flash of mood change, the blond gave Thomas a tight hug. A growl built in Ben's throat but was quickly suppressed when Anthony released Thomas and hugged him instead.

Skinny arms wrapped around him like a cozy blanket as a feeling of intense well-being oozed through his body like a narcotic. The man smelled like a living forest, moist soil, green fields, and old oak trees. Anthony smelled like home, even though home was more cold, snow-covered woods than toasty warm forests. Ben dipped his head in the beauty's neck and breathed. Stress he didn't know he was holding left his body in a gush, leaving him calm and almost dizzy with relief.

A low, dangerous growl broke his calm.

"I'd suggest you let go of my mate before I rip off your arms and beat you with them." The voice was so deep and calm he could almost feel the homicidal rage hidden beneath the words.

The blond wiggled out of his arms. "Relax, snookums. I was just greeting Thomas's mate."

Watching the sweet, beautiful man walk up to the calm psychotic twice his size made Ben's fingers twitch with the urge to yank Anthony to safety. The threatening man's sleeveless shirt exposed a set of mile-wide shoulders and arms bulging with tight muscles. His grey eyes were the color of an Alaskan winter sky and just as warm. Ben's protective instincts rose up until he saw the man turn and give the sleek blond a look of total adoration. It was like watching an iceberg melt before his eyes. One massive arm wrapped around Anthony cradling him close in an obviously tender hold.

Anthony smiled. Standing on his tiptoes he placed a soft kiss on one granite hard cheek.

"I'll pay you back for the snookums comment," the giant said.

The blond looked completely unperturbed. He blithely patted his lover on one bulging bicep while batting his beautiful eyes artfully. "I'll look forward to it."

Ben watched the whole thing, fascinated. The power pouring off the male was alpha strong, but it was obvious who was in charge of that relationship.

One large hand reached out to him, he tentatively took it. "I'm Silver Moon, the alpha of the Moon pack. Thomas is my right hand man."

"Benjamin."

A quirk of the alpha's brow had him confessing. "I'm a lone wolf."

Silver stiffened. "Why?"

"We were planning to go talk about his

status when your mate stopped us to plead for fewer bodyguards and to grope our bodies." Thomas reached over and grabbed Ben's hand to drag him down the hall.

Ben was chilled his mate would throw Anthony literally to the wolves. He dug in his heels, bracing himself to jump in. The alpha might kill him, but he felt oddly protective of the pretty man who smelled like a forest. Instead of growling Silver threw back his head and laughed. "You two go ahead and have your discussion while I explain to my headstrong mate why he needs so many guards." The alpha growled at the slim blond who barely came to his shoulder.

"You-you're not going to hurt him, are you?" Ben couldn't help it. He feared for the smaller man's safety next to his huge mate. The alpha didn't appear angry but Ben had enough experience with alphas to know their tempers changed with the wind.

Anthony gave him a big smile. "You're very sweet, but Silver would never hurt me. Welcome to the pack."

Silver growled. "You're not allowed to welcome people to my pack. I'm the alpha; I get to welcome or not."

Wow, this looked like a real fight. The

welcoming expression left the blond as the shimmering gold eyes turned solid before turning back to his mate. He could've sworn he saw lightning flash in them before Anthony turned, but he figured it was a trick of the hall lighting.

"Shit," Thomas whispered behind him. Ben was slowly pulled away from the bickering pair. He could tell the other man was trying to remove him from the line of fire.

"Oh it's your pack is it? I guess I'm just a pet accessory. I foolishly thought we were partners in this relationship. You just let me know what your decision is then, big man, and I'll decide whether you're welcome in *my* bed." With a frightening calmness rivaling the rage of his mate seconds before, Anthony slammed the door to the apartment he recently left.

"Fuck." The alpha glared at Thomas. "He better fucking *be* your mate because there's no way I can go tell *mine* that I didn't approve him." Leveling an icy glare at the pair, Silver followed the smaller man's wake into the apartment.

"Well, that was enlightening," Thomas said with a wide smile at Ben. "Looks like Anthony can sense mates."

"Why does he smell so good?" Ben

didn't want to give the wrong impression, but damn. "Don't take this wrong. I mean you smell great, but he smells amazing. Not mate amazing, but amazing."

Thomas nodded and gave him a knowing grin. "Anthony's mother is a forest witch. I still haven't found out what his father is. Just a word of warning, smell him at a distance. That's what we all do."

Ben nodded. "Distance, got it."

He was positive he didn't want to be on the bad side of the alpha even if he didn't end up joining the pack.

* * * *

Thomas walked down the hall to his suite in silence. With Anthony's approval he knew his mate would be accepted into the pack. There was normally a meeting to determine if a new mate would fit in with the pack hierarchy or if they would need to join the other wolf's pack. Sometimes it was a matter of whether a new personality fit into the group dynamic. He had a feeling Anthony would short track the entire process. After all, Silver didn't want estrangement from his beautiful man and his mate was more than a little strong-willed. The alpha mate might not be a wolf but he was powerful in his own right.

Feeling better about the relationship by the second, Thomas led the cute redhead to his door.

"Each of us has a suite. The higher in the hierarchy we are, the better the accommodations, but no one has bad rooms. Some prefer to live in their own places outside the pack house, but we encourage as many as possible to live here. It's harder to protect everyone if they're scattered around town.

Ben nodded. "Makes sense. I imagine it's difficult to keep track of everyone in a big city. Is there more than one pack here?"

"There are four packs in the area, but the Moon pack is the only one in the city and Silver supervises the entire Northwest. Most consider him the strongest wolf in the United States. Anthony, who you just met, is an architect and is currently building a hotel to host out-of-town paranaturals."

"Clever."

Thomas nodded. "We're pretty proud of him. He was reluctant to be Silver's mate at first because he lost a lover to a heart attack some years ago, but he's settled in well. As you can see they still have some power issues to work out. We won't have that kind of problem."

He watched his mate puff up his chest

like an animal trying to make himself bigger. "And why is that?" Ben's eyes took on a challenging shine.

Damn if that didn't make his dick stand up and take notice.

"Because although I'm the larger of the two of us, I think we're pretty evenly paired power wise. The problem with the alpha and his mate is that they have different types of magic. Silver has issues with having a strong mate who looks like a good wind will knock him on his ass, which is why he usually has a retinue of bodyguards surrounding Anthony. I don't even want to know where they were this evening, Silver's going to have some harsh words for someone."

Thomas could tell by the pleased expression on Ben's face that they were going to be fine. He rarely met someone he meshed with so quickly. Seeing the man in Ned's clutches had almost unhinged him. It was fortunate the other werewolf had released his hold on the redhead quickly. He made a mental note to talk to Silver about Ned's progressively aggressive behavior. They would have to bar him from the club if he kept it up. As much as the place was for werekin to hook up, it was also a place they were supposed to feel safe. They couldn't have anyone there who scared the other customers. Ben's panicky expression had Thomas rushing to save him even before he knew they were mates.

He opened the door to his apartment and, after hanging up their jackets, indicated to his mate to proceed to the couch. Thomas kept his promise and left the door unlocked. It wasn't like anyone was going to interrupt them anyway.

"Sit down, honey."

He knew his gaze was feral but he was determined to find out more about his mate before he pinned him down, marked him, and made sure they were bound for eternity. Ben sank down into the soft cushions, his eyes wide with caution. "This must be nice to nap on," he said petting the soft fabric. Thomas had a brief vision of the man doing the same to him. The redhead's fingers were long, elegant, and he wanted them wrapped around his cock more than he'd ever wanted anything else in his life. He pushed back those thoughts using a great deal of restraint. "I want to learn a little more about you. If we're going to be mates we should find out about our likes, dislikes, how old you are, why you left your pack, and what you do for a living."

Ben winced. "I don't suppose we could kiss first and answer questions later."

Thomas laughed. Scooting over, he slid a hand up his mate's leg. "Tell you what, pretty. For every question you answer I'll give you one kiss." He knew it was probably a terrible idea, but the thought of not touching the other man within the next few seconds was killing him. Both his human and wolf sides wanted the man with an unprecedented need.

"Fair enough," Ben agreed, quickly. "I'm twenty-five."

He would be lying if he didn't hope his future mate would've started with something more personal. He gave the answer the response it deserved.

Thomas leaned over and gave Ben's cheek a peck.

"That wasn't a kiss."

"A small answer gets you a small kiss. Besides, you're just a baby. I've got a hundred years on you."

"Wow." Ben's eyes went wide, making Thomas wonder if age was going to be a problem between them. In general, werekin didn't worry about age differences because they lived long lives. What would be an insurmountable age gap in a human couple wasn't worth mentioning between werekin.

"Does the age difference bother you?"

"No. I was just surprised."

"Yeah, that's real convincing."

Ben rolled his eyes. "Give me a moment to adjust, all right. Not everyone learns their mate is so much older than them."

Mate. The word made Thomas smile.

He leaned over, sliding his fingers into Ben's hair gripping the man's head in a firm hold. "I believe I owe you another kiss to convince you of my worthiness as a potential mate."

"Yes, I believe you do."

This time the kiss wasn't chaste, light, or brief. This time Thomas searched for the size and shape of Ben's tonsils. He took Ben's mouth like a parched man seeking the last drop of water in a desert.

One kiss blurred into two, until the sexy redhead lay shirtless beneath him. Thomas nipped and sucked the smaller man's nipples. Pleased with the reaction, he kept it up, palming the ridge in his mate's pants as Ben squirmed beneath his touch.

"Fuck questions, I need to feel you around me." Thomas froze as an unwelcome thought entered his mind. "You will bottom, right? I don't mind switching back and forth in the future, but right now I need to claim you." He barely breathed as he waited for his mate's answer.

"I won't always be on the bottom, but for tonight I'm all yours." Ben leaned back and let Thomas's hot mouth take control.

Unable to resist the need for bare skin to skin contact, Thomas's touch was sure and confident as he stripped off his mate's clothes in swift, economical movements before removing his own. He barely got a glimpse of smooth white skin, with a sexy sprinkling of red hair, before he covered the younger man with his body.

"Hey! I didn't get to look," his mate protested.

"Why bother to look when it's so much better to feel?" Thomas growled, sliding his body across Ben's and sending shivers of need through his smaller frame.

He was careful not to put his full weight on the younger man. He didn't want to crush his newly found mate. He wanted to bond with him.

* * * *

Thomas's cock felt long and hard against Ben's stomach, its silky head trailing wet kisses across his naked flesh. Unlike his partner, Ben's body was relatively hair free with only a light sprinkling on his arms and legs. A part of his half-breed status, it always caused uncomfortable staring by the other wolves on full moon pack night, except from Dillon whose gaze was never uncomfortable, just needy. His eyes made Ben hard, which was why he always tried to change away from the other man. It was difficult enough to make the change when you were only half wolf; it was much harder if your concentration was on your cock.

"You feel so good." Thomas's low voice brought Ben away from thoughts of his previous pack. Now was the time for a new start. A new start with this amazing man who not only wanted him for a mate, but wanted him in other ways as well. Dillon was in the past where he needed to stay. Regrets never did anyone any good.

Ben clenched his stomach and rubbed his cock along Thomas's. The other werekin jerked. "Keep that up and there won't be any question about who's topping. I'll come before I get inside you."

Chuckling, Ben grabbed Thomas's tight ass, pulling him closer while giving in to temptation to kiss those fabulous lips. Lips slid together and mouths opened to allow tongues to entwine. Ben's cock pulsed in reaction to the feel and taste of the other man. Thomas gripped him tight around the base, pulling away from the kiss.

"No coming yet. I want to be inside when you do."

"Then you'd better hurry."

Thomas released him before jumping to his feet. He held out a hand to help Ben up, a good thing since all of his brainpower abandoned him. The other werewolf held all of his attention and he couldn't think past the next touch.

"Bedroom. Lube." Those two words had Ben jumping to join his mate.

"We can do the couch another time," he agreed.

A low, dirty chuckle came from the sophisticated-looking man. "Count on it."

Still holding hands, they all but sprinted to the other room. A dark wooden four-poster bed with an embossed leather headboard was the starring attraction. Ben gave it a cursory glance before leaping for the mattress. Lying there he crooked a finger at his mate.

"Come here, gorgeous."

"Who knew such a shy, pretty thing like you would be an animal in the bedroom?"

"I'm not shy," Ben said with a smile, "I'm just not an asshole. Besides, we both know I'm an animal a lot more places than the bed, but we can start here."

After giving him a heated glance, Thomas reached into a bedside drawer and pulled out a bottle of lube.

Ben looked at the label. "Nice," he said with approval.

"Only the best for my mate."

He doubted it was waiting there the entire time for him to wander by, but not wanting to ruin the mood, he beckoned his lover closer. Ben didn't care who used to share Thomas's bed, there would be no one else from now on. That's how mates worked, at least in Alaska. He'd have to find out what the mores were here. Though to be truthful he didn't care. He wasn't going to share Thomas. He'd have to find a good way to break the news to the sexy man.

Eventually.

"Come show me what you can do with your fancy lube."

With a wicked smile Thomas joined his mate on the bed.

* * * *

Looking at the beautiful man's pale skin

against his navy blue covers almost had Thomas coming all over the bedding without ever touching the jewel lying there. Damn, he'd thought the man adorable in the bar. Here, without any clothing, he was so much more. Without any covering he could glimpse the predator lying beneath the surface of the slim body and, for the first time, he was turned on by another wolf's power.

Hoping Ben didn't notice his shaking fingers, Thomas popped open the lube cap, spreading the liquid liberally across his fingers. Without a word Ben rolled onto his stomach before sliding onto his hands and knees and presenting himself beautifully.

Thomas almost came. Again. He gave a rough laugh, unable to help the bubble of joy building in his throat.

"If you keep that up, it will be the shortest mating of all time."

Ben laughed. "Hurry up or I'll finish without you."

He could see the redhead reaching for his long, gorgeous cock.

Discarding caution, Thomas leapt. "Gotcha."

His mate wiggled beneath him. "You had me before."

He smacked Ben on the ass. "Don't ruin my fun."

"Yes, sir."

He snorted. Thomas couldn't remember the last time he'd had fun in the bedroom; sweaty hot sex, yes, but not fun.

Easing his first finger inside Ben's tight hole he gave his mate a moment to relax, pumping in and out while he waited for the smaller man to adjust.

"Another," Ben grunted.

Thomas slid another finger in, scissoring the two until the younger man loosened up. "Ready for my cock."

Ben nodded. "Yeah, give it to me."

Pressing a kiss on one freckled shoulder, Thomas aligned the tip of his penis with his mate's hole and slowly pressed in until his balls snuggled up against Ben's. Simultaneous sighs came from the lovers, triggering a round of giggles.

"Stop that," Thomas growled. "You'll make me come." Being inside a man while laughing caused the oddest sensations. Smiling against his mate's back, he slowly pumped his hips until Ben screamed at him.

"Faster!"

Eager to oblige, he shoved himself

quicker inside the younger man, letting nature and the bliss of finding his mate determine his speed and depth. Despite wanting to prolong the experience, Thomas could feel he was close. Reaching around, he gripped his mate's cock, giving the man something to rub against while still moving inside him.

His fangs dropped and, giving into his wolf's needs, Thomas bit down on the tender skin between neck and shoulder.

Ben screamed. Wetness coated Thomas's hand as the smaller man's hole clenched around him, pulling him into orgasm. Howling, he pumped his seed into his mate's tight ass. Together the pair collapsed on the bed. Thomas barely remembered to fall to one side in time to avoid crushing his mate. With careful movements he slid out of Ben and licked at the wound he'd created.

"Mine, my mate," he said into the sudden quiet of the room. He could feel their hearts beating together, a wild rhythm of two creatures desperately trying to become one.

"Wow." Ben's whisper brought a wide smile to his face.

"Sometimes it pays to be with someone with experience," Thomas said modestly.

"I don't want to know where you got all

that experience." Ben's voice was firm, but also a little sad.

Pulling his mate close, Thomas cuddled him in his arms. "Don't give it a thought, my sweet. You know with our mating I'll never have anyone else again."

"Good. I didn't know if your pack worked that way or not. I was trying to figure out a way to break the news to you that you were no longer single." Ticklish fingers tangled with his chest hair. "'Cause if you did fool around with someone else I'd make sure that was the last thing you did."

"Ouch." A portion of his chest hair was now between Ben's fingers and no longer attached.

"Possessive wolf," he said, affectionately rubbing noses with his mate. "Let me go get a cloth to wipe us down."

A few minutes later, cleaned up and cuddling, the two werewolves fell asleep for the first time as mates.

CHAPTER TWO

Ben slid onto the bar stool and gave the bartender a smile.

"Hey, Dare, can I get a glass of water?"

"Sure thing, Ben." The friendly bartender poured him a glass, gave him a wink and moved on. A typical Saturday, even before four in the afternoon, the bar was jumping with visitors and their guests. Ben had finished up with his customers earlier that day and was now waiting for his mate.

The last two weeks had passed in a blur of hot sex and bonding. Sleeping in Thomas's arms was the highlight of his day. It never ceased to surprise him that the other wolf was a snuggler. Sometimes it got too hot with all the heat his mate put out but he'd happily sleep in an inferno if it kept the big man close.

Thomas was everything he'd ever wanted in a mate; strong, sweet, and respectful of Ben having a brain of his own. They didn't have any battles for who was the bigger alpha. It was a bonding of equals. If occasionally his heart yearned for the wolf he left behind, well, he would never tell.

Drinking his water, Ben felt as if

everything was right in his world. He had yet to tell Thomas what he did for a living. He'd just wait until the man threw the bank statements across the room again before admitting he was an accountant. From the growl in his lover's voice when he left, it shouldn't take much longer.

"There you are," a familiar voice growled in his ear.

Ben spun around on his stool, shock making him stare mutely for a long moment. "D-Dillon! What are you doing here?" Without any will of his own, Ben's eyes dragged up and down the wolf he'd always considered the epitome of werekin. Comfortably over six feet, Dillon was all muscle and attitude. His job as a landscape architect kept him fit and firm while his brilliant mind was just as captivating. Lost in a pair of dark green eyes, it took a moment before the other wolf's words sank in. "Why are you here?"

"I'm claiming my mate."

Pain ripped through Ben. He knew once he mated with Thomas, Dillon was history, but the thought of the man he wanted all his life claiming another was almost more than he could take.

What a selfish ass he was.

"Congratulations on finding your mate," he choked out. It was a bitter pill to swallow; even thoughts of his lover weren't quite enough to dull the sharp stabbing ache in his heart.

"Thank you. I'm sure we'll be very happy together."

Ben searched for a polite phrase of support but it was beyond him. As much as he wanted Dillon happy, he'd gladly rip off the head of the bastard who had the gall to attract the man he'd always secretly wanted as his own.

His mind spinning, Ben was taken by surprise when large hands plucked him from his stool. Firm, masterful lips took him in a show of complete domination before he could object. Long buried desires came to the surface as Ben melted in the larger werewolf's hands. He tasted so damn good and smelled like sunshine.

"Get your fucking hands off my mate," the words were said in a low growl, but even so, they cut through the noise of the club like a hot knife through butter.

* * * *

Dillon let go of his mate and turned to confront this new threat, tucking Ben protectively behind him.

"Stay there, honey."

For some reason, his words inflamed the

strange werewolf.

"Don't you honey him. He's mine," the other werewolf growled. He could see fangs descending as rage took over reason.

"He's my mate." Dillon didn't care about the other man's posturing. There was no way he was giving up Benjamin. He'd tracked the kid halfway across the world, he wasn't going to hand him over to this werewolf-come-lately. It didn't matter to him if the man looked like a model in his well-cut suit, a suit that highlighted the other man's delicious body.

Ben growled behind him. "Dillon, don't you hurt my mate."

"Mate?" he shouted as his heart skipped a beat. "He's not your mate. I am."

"Not in this lifetime, good luck with the next," the strange wolf piped up with a smirk.

Dillon's hands shifted into claws as he let out a loud growl. "No one takes what is mine." Pouncing, he ripped through the other man's shirt, shredding through cloth to get at the man hiding inside. The urge to rip out his enemy's heart burned through him. How dare this newcomer claim what was his? There was no doubt in his mind that he would have to kill this interloper. His wolf demanded blood.

He barely dodged in time to avoid the

other man's shifted claw attack. Dillon growled and with an impressive show of reflexes, grabbed the other werewolf by the throat and slammed him against the bar. In a show of domination, Dillon lowered his head and bit the other man, his teeth sinking into the strange werewolf's neck. His concentration was thrown off when his cock hardened against the other man. The wolf smelled like cocoa and berries, happy memories from his childhood. His fangs retracted in surprise.

Taking advantage of his distraction, the stranger lifted Dillon up and slammed him onto the hard dance floor. He heard something snap inside, pain screamed through his system sending his body into convulsions as he fought the change. Shifting was any werewolf's reaction to damage, but he didn't want to lose the time it would take to shift. He couldn't leave Ben unprotected.

"Don't hurt him," Ben shouted. Dillon was pleased to hear concern in his mate's voice even as pain splintered his head and his world greyed out.

He was changing.

Dillon blinked awake as a deep voice growled, "What the hell is going on?"

Lying on the floor, he watched as the

biggest werewolf he'd ever seen stalked into his vision. The werewolf was followed by a slim, beautiful blond man who had a slight smile on his face as if he found the whole thing incredibly amusing. Did he glow? Nah. Must be the blow to his head.

"Aren't you a pretty wolf," the blond said in a singsong tone. He would've growled at the other man but he smelled so good and he scratched. Yesss, right there. His leg thumped from the attention.

"Stop petting him," the alpha ordered. The big shifter leaned down to grab the good-smelling man and Dillon snapped his teeth at him aggressively.

The alpha growled. Instinct had Dillon rolling over and showing his belly. He tried to send an apologetic look at the smaller man who petted him on his head before going to stand next to the alpha wolf.

"You always have to cause trouble, don't you?" the big wolf said, planting a gentle kiss on the smaller man's cheek.

"Yep."

"Dillon," Ben whispered, sliding to the floor to cradle the wolf's head in his lap. His eyes glowed in the dim club light. Ben's eyes were his best feature. Warm and expressive, they let anyone watching know what the younger man was feeling. Dillon turned his head, pressing his nose close to his mate's crotch, inhaling the delicious smell of arousal. The human in him whimpered with need.

He could kill himself for missing the claiming. He hadn't known the exact date and his parents had purposely arranged for him to be out of town on pack business. Father was still recovering from the wounds Dillon inflicted when he found out his mate had not only left the pack, but the state as well. It had taken a while to get things in order, but luckily Ben had left word with a few friends as to where he was heading. From there Dillon was able to track his erstwhile man only find him mated to another.

"Well that was interesting," amusement filled the blond's voice as he helped the other werewolf off the floor and handed him a cloth to hold to his bloody neck.

"Thomas, what the hell is going on?" the alpha demanded.

"That man is trying to steal my mate." Thomas pointed at Dillon.

* * * *

Ben watched the entire scene like he was a spectator in his own life. Somehow it didn't feel real. He was jolted from his fog when

Anthony smiled down at him. "Hey, Ben, you found your other mate. Congratulations."

Busy inhaling Anthony's scrumptious smell, it took a moment for the man's words to sink in. "Other mate?"

"Well, yeah, most fae need more than one mate."

He dropped the bomb nonchalantly, as if he didn't just change Ben's world view. "What do you mean, fae? My mother was human."

Ben stood up, carefully laying Dillon's head on the floor. He wanted to be on his feet for this discussion. Thomas wrapped his arm around Ben for moral support. He was grateful for the comfort but more than a little confused. Confused and excited. What if he could have them both? It was greedy and wrong… but oh, so tempting.

Anthony laughed, a light tinkling sound that danced around the room like sparkling sunlight. "If she told you that, she lied. You're at least half fae. I can always recognize fae blood."

"You mean he's not a full wolf?" Thomas stared at Ben as if trying to spot any genetic defects. "You can shift though, right?" he asked after a long pause where Ben felt sicker and sicker.

Ben nodded. He tried to pull away from

Thomas but the other wolf wasn't letting go.

There was a crackling sound as Dillon shifted. It only took a few moments because his childhood friend was a strong wolf. In no time at all the dark-haired man was shaking his head and standing up to face them. His green eyes focused on Thomas, or more specifically, his arm around Ben.

"I know I'm Ben's mate, and if you think you're Ben's mate then we have a problem. I'm not giving him up." Ben saw the fanatical light in Dillon's eyes and knew there would be trouble unless he laid some ground rules.

"Forget about it Dillon," he warned. "I know that look. If something happens to Thomas I'm holding you responsible."

"Everyone settle down. Let's go to my office and talk about this. We don't need another fight in the club. You're lucky it isn't during our busy hour or I'd throw all of your asses out." Silver led the way through a sea of interested onlookers to a door at the back of the club. Inside was a spacious office with a big desk, a pair of leather sofas, and a trio of leather chairs. Everything was done in rich brown tones. Silver sat on one couch, tugging his smaller mate onto his lap.

Dillon took one of the large leather

chairs. Thomas took another one. They both looked at Ben expectantly. He joined the alpha pair on the couch, pulling Anthony's feet onto his lap. He needed the comfort of touch, even if he barely knew the other man. Neither of his potential mates looked like they were in the cuddling mood, and to choose one over the other at this point could end in carnage. Needing the reassurance of bare skin, he automatically slipped off Anthony's sandals and started massaging his feet.

"I'll give you about six hundred years to stop that," Anthony said, closing his eyes with a sigh.

"Don't go to sleep, sweetness. You were going to tell us how you knew about Ben."

Anthony leaned his head against the alpha's chest. "Hmm. My father is half fae. I'm barely a quarter fae, but there's always something that gives them away. With Ben it's his eyes. I've only seen that color in the fae court."

"When were you at the fae court?" Silver asked in a deceptively mild voice, but Ben could see the alpha narrow his eyes as if getting ready for an interrogation.

He jumped in, instinctively trying to protect Anthony. "Aren't we getting off track?

What am I going to do? I don't think these two are willing to share me." He glanced at the hard faces of his mates. Matching expressions of anger flashed back at him. "See."

Anthony shrugged. "Tough. They can either share you or be alone. I've never heard of a fae who could live with less than one mate."

A look of horror crossed the alpha's face. Ben saw him swallow. "Does that mean you'll need a second mate?" Silver asked, not entirely hiding his panic.

Laughing, Anthony turned his head and gave his lover a kiss. "I'm only a quarter, sweetheart. I have all the mate I can handle."

"Good." Silver hugged his mate tight. "Very good."

Thomas jumped to his feet and confronted the alpha. "So you think it's all right for me to share, even though you'd kill anyone who even thought of touching your mate?"

With a soft kiss, Silver lifted his mate to his feet before standing himself. "I can't kill everyone who thinks of touching Anthony or we wouldn't have anyone left in our pack." Powerful grey eyes examined the three of them. Ben felt the twitchy compulsion to show his belly to the big alpha. Damn, he was strong.

"Like my mate said. You can either cope

or you can join the pack as a tri-mate. It has happened before, but as far as I know it hasn't happened in the last hundred years or so. The three of you must decide what you want to do and all three of you have to agree if you're going to join the pack. I won't have dissention. Understand?"

The hair along Ben's arms rose. He wanted to get Anthony alone to ask him more about the fae, but he could tell by the look his mates were exchanging that now wasn't the time. Fae blood could explain his insane need to protect Anthony. Blood called to blood.

Thomas gave his alpha a bow. "We need to discuss this. Thank you for your advice, Silver." He gave a lower bow to Anthony with a smile. "And for your input, alpha mate."

Anthony blew him a kiss.

Ben looked at Anthony for a moment, curious as to why he didn't hug Dillon and welcome him to the family.

Dillon also gave a bow and a slight head tilt, exposing his throat to the mated pair. "I also thank you for your advice and the option to join your pack. I hadn't really thought past getting Ben. We have much to discuss." Dillon stepped forward. Taking Anthony's hand he placed a kiss on the back of it. "Of course, I have never been with a pack that had such a pretty alpha mate."

Silver took his mate's hand from Dillon and rubbed off the other wolf's scent with his thumb. Anthony's eyes sparkled as he turned to Ben. "I'd keep an eye out for this one honey, he's smooth."

The alpha pair left, but not before Silver gave Dillon a warning look over his shoulder.

CHAPTER THREE

Thomas couldn't believe things went so bad so fast. Just an hour earlier he was dreaming of joining his mate at the bar for a few drinks before bed, now not only was that ruined but he might have just gained an extra wolf to his mating. Not that Dillon was unattractive, but he wasn't Thomas's mate and it would take all the control he had to not snap the fucker's neck as soon as Ben's back was turned. The thought of the tall, muscular man touching Ben made him queasy and angry in turn.

"What are we going to do?"

Dillon sat back down on the leather seat. "We need to figure out a way to bond together. I'm not giving Ben up. He's mine and if he insists on being yours too, then I say we petition for tri-mate. We'd best do it here because our Alaskan pack won't acknowledge a tri-mate. Hell, they won't even acknowledge a gay mated pair."

Thomas' eyes met Dillon's. For the first time it struck him how pretty the other man's green eyes were. They were mesmerizing, with little flakes of gold inside a forest of green.

Still he couldn't stop his smirk. "Ben

doesn't have to petition. He was already accepted."

Dillon stared at Ben. "How is that possible? There isn't a full moon until next month."

Ben smiled. "Anthony decided I would make a good pack member and welcomed me."

"B-but he's not a wolf."

Dillon's confusion was almost cute. Thomas uncharitably enjoyed the other man's distress. "Anthony may be an architect and a non-werekin, but anyone can see who's in charge of that relationship."

Dillon snorted. "I did get that impression. Wait what's his last name."

"Carrow."

"Wow. I thought he looked familiar. Have you ever been to The Carrow Hotel?"

Thomas shook his head. "No, but I've heard it's amazing. Are you an architect?"

Dillon shook his head. "Landscape design."

"If you stay, maybe Anthony can find work for you," Ben suggested.

"Or Silver," Thomas said with a smile. "He's always looking for more people to guard his mate."

"Is he in trouble?" Dillon asked, a

concerned frown creasing his handsome face. His expression showed he would be willing to be a guard if that was what the alpha wanted. Thomas had the sinking feeling the other man would be a good addition to the pack. If Dillon weren't after Thomas's mate, he knew the pair of them would've been friends. As it was he wanted the man gone. Dead would be better, but he'd settle for elsewhere. Unfortunately, it looked like he wasn't going to get his wish.

Ever.

"No, but he has a new project that has him working with vamps and other paranaturals. Silver has a fear one of them will try to take off with his treasure."

"It's a valid fear," Ben said. "He's kind and beautiful, anyone would be anxious if he was their mate."

Thomas and Dillon growled together.

"Oh, please. Like you didn't notice," Ben said, rolling his eyes.

"Let's stay on track. How are we going to share a mate?" Thomas didn't want to share Ben at all, but if the only other choice were to have his mate forever missing his other half then he would do whatever was needed to keep Ben happy.

"I could get a place near here until I'm

accepted as a member. We could take turns bonding with Ben and cementing our claim. I'll take him with me now since I'm sure you've already claimed him as your mate."

"You aren't taking him anywhere," Thomas said.

"I grew up with him, he's mine," Dillon replied.

Fuck that.

"Then you should've claimed him when you had the chance instead of letting him go thousands of miles away to find another mate."

Thomas saw the punch coming and ducked out of the way in time, taking the force of the hit on his shoulder.

"That's enough," Ben shouted.

Thomas and Dillon froze.

"Stop fighting over me. If you are both my mates then you need to learn to share. Thomas, I think it would be a good idea if I go back with Dillon to his hotel and talk."

"No. There's no way I'm going to let a stranger leave with my mate." Thomas held up his hand to stave off the protests. "No offense, Dillon, but I don't know you and I'm not going to just hand Ben over. You can sleep on the couch, but I want to be there when you talk to our mate. I don't know what happened between you, and if we're all going to have some kind of relationship I want the details."

Ben bit his lip. The poor dear kept looking back and forth between them like a dog trying to decide who his master was.

Dillon glared at Thomas before letting out a sigh. "I hate to admit it, but I wouldn't let you walk out with Ben either. Okay, I'll get my bag out of the car and come back here for our little talk."

When Dillon left, Ben threw himself into Thomas's arms. "I'm so sorry, Thomas. I didn't think he would come after me. When he didn't show for the claiming I thought we were done."

Thomas swallowed the lump in his throat. "Do you love him?"

Ben nodded averting his eyes from Thomas's probing gaze.

"Look at me, honey." There were tears in the redhead's eyes. "You can't help who you love."

Ben laid his head on Thomas shoulder holding on tight. "But I love you, too."

He stroked his mate's back to calm the shaking he could feel through the thin shirt. "We'll figure something out. I'm not letting you go." He gave Ben a little shake. "Understand?"

Ben nodded, giving a watery chuckle.

Before he could say anything else, the door swung back open. Dillon's gaze flattened at the sight of them embracing.

"Get used to it," Thomas said. "If we're all going to be together you'll see me do a great deal more than hold him."

Dillon nodded. "True enough, but it doesn't mean I have to like it."

Ben stepped out of Thomas's embrace, but softened the mood by placing a gentle kiss on his lips.

A growl came from Dillon. When the pair turned to face him he shrugged, his cheeks glowing pink. "Sorry, instinct."

Thomas let it go. At least it looked like Dillon was trying.

* * * *

Dillon watched the pair. It was difficult resisting the urge to rip Ben away from the other werewolf. God knew Thomas was being completely decent about the whole thing. If he wanted to, the other wolf could have used his connections and had Dillon tossed out of the city. That alpha looked badass enough to do it. Maybe even ban him for life, or kill him quietly and hide the body. All things he'd seriously consider in a similar situation. If he had bonded with Ben first, he wouldn't be as gracious.

He carefully assessed Ben and was both pleased and disturbed to see the young werewolf looking so well. In the back of his mind he'd imagined the younger wolf pining for him and grateful for Dillon hunting him down. He hadn't imagined Ben perfectly happy with a handsome mate of his own. Other than death, it was the worst scenario possible.

"Ben, I want you to know I planned to be there for the claiming, but my parents sent me out of town."

"They never liked me," Ben said in a quiet voice. He sat on the couch, pulling his knees to his chest.

Thomas settled on the couch beside him, lifting Ben onto his lap to comfort the young werewolf. Dillon yearned to be the one stroking the golden-red head, but he knew now wasn't the time.

"I don't understand what a claiming is," Thomas piped up.

"You don't have claiming ceremonies here?"

Thomas shook his head. "When you know at first sniff if someone is your mate, why would you need a ceremony?"

Dillon shrugged. "That's just the way we always did it. When a werekin reaches the age of twenty-five they're eligible for the ceremony. If no one claims them, they can go lone wolf or stick around and hope someone joins the pack that'll match him or her." He turned an imploring gaze on the redhead. "Ben, why didn't you wait for me? You knew I was going to claim you."

That was the question that haunted his dreams. What if, after all he'd gone through, Ben didn't really want him?

Ben stood up, patting Thomas's leg in an affectionate gesture. It didn't help Dillon to see all the extra touches of affection heaped onto Thomas and not even one kiss for him.

"I didn't know you were going to claim me. I hoped, but when you weren't there for the ceremony I figured it was your way of letting me down easy. Your father told me you chose to go on this trip during the Claiming. I thought maybe it was your way of saying you didn't want me without actually saying the words."

Dillon stared at his gorgeous mate for a long moment. "How could you not know that I wanted you? Since the first day I saw you, there hasn't been a breath I take that I didn't want to breathe your scent, not a voice I heard that I didn't prefer it to be yours. You are everything to me."

He took Ben's hands and slid to his knees, trying to hide the panic thudding in his chest as he looked up at the man who was his world. "I can't live without you. Please be my mate."

Tears shone in Ben's eyes. With gentle pressure he tugged at Dillon's hands, urging him to his feet. "I'm sorry you can't be my only mate, Dillon, but if you're willing to share I would love to have you as part of my tri-mating."

A watery laugh left Dillon's throat as he wrapped his arms around his love, taking a deep breath to inhale his mate's sweet scent. The aroma of lemony hair product mixed with lust and love went straight to his cock.

"I want you." All the love Dillon yearned for glowed in the young werewolf's beautiful eyes.

He felt the other man approach but didn't take his eyes off Ben.

"You're going to have to deal with me sometime." Thomas's dry voice broke into the moment.

Dillon sighed and turned his head to look at the other werewolf, breaking the intense gaze with his love. For the first time he really looked at Thomas. Looked beyond the sleek exterior and into his hazel eyes and saw the same worries reflected there that he felt himself.

"Are you willing to share him?"

Thomas nodded. "Not eager, but willing. Let's take this to the bedroom and see if we can share. If our wolves can't share then one of us will have to go."

He didn't need to say it was Dillon who would go, after all it was Thomas's pack. He just nodded, and for the first time in his life found himself in the weaker position. A strong wolf in his pack, it was difficult for him to defer to another, but for Ben he was willing to try.

"Last chance, Ben. You can still come back with me."

Really, he couldn't help it.

Ben gave him a sad smile. "I already bonded with Thomas."

"Shit."

Now there was no way to take it back. Once bonded, wolves couldn't be apart from each other for more than a few days. One of the reasons mated wolves always traveled together.

"Nice try," Thomas smirked.

"Like you wouldn't have."

"That's why I didn't punch you."

Dillon smiled. He had a feeling Thomas might understand him better than Ben did. A strong wolf, but a sensitive human, not a combination desired in the Alaskan pack. He didn't think it would be a problem in this new pack Ben had found. After all, the alpha mate was a delicate looking creature with no werekin blood. If the head alpha didn't mind a sensitive man for a mate he wouldn't mind a gentle half wolf in the pack.

Thinking over different scenarios he followed the pair into the bedroom, stopping in stunned surprise.

"Damn. That's the biggest bed I've ever seen."

Thomas gave it a long look as if he hadn't seen it before. "When I bought a new bed last year, I purchased the largest one they had. Now I wonder if it was because I had a foreshadowing of the three of us. Sight runs in my family. I had thought it missed me, but now I'm not so sure."

"Maybe not," Dillon agreed. Thomas was a large man, but average for werekin. Ben was on the smaller side, so the two of them didn't need that much space even if they moved in their sleep. A knot unfurled in his stomach. If Thomas foresaw needing more space then maybe everything was going to work out all right.

Thomas stripped to his underwear.

Dillon took a moment to admire Thomas's lean form before walking to Ben and pulling off the younger werewolf's shirt in one smooth motion. He felt a motion by his feet. Looking down, he found Thomas on his knees removing Ben's shoes.

The position of the mostly naked man kneeling at his feet made his cock stand up and take notice. Thomas's pretty hazel eyes sparkled. "Just because you and I aren't mates doesn't mean we can't explore each other. After all, we'll be together for a long time."

"Ohhh, could the two of you kiss? That would be sooo hot," Ben cooed.

Thomas stood up, positioning Ben between them. A cautious look entered his eyes, a feeling reflected by Dillon.

"Are you sure, honey?" Dillon asked. "It won't feel weird to you?"

Ben shrugged. "Like Thomas said, we're going to have a long life together. I can't imagine us sharing a bed for hundreds of years and the two of you not touching. It's unnatural."

Dillon felt Ben's clever fingers slide into his hair. "Kiss me first, maybe it will be easier with my taste on your lips."

"Now that's something I can agree with." Dillon wrapped his arms around Ben, pulling the hard, young body tight against his. Without giving him a chance to change his mind, he took his mate's mouth with all the desperate longing built up since the entire mating business started. He tried to convey through his touch just how much he wanted this to work. There was nothing he wouldn't do for his mate.

The first kiss ran into a second when Ben responded with more enthusiasm than Dillon expected. The type of enthusiasm he'd thought to find only in his dreams. This was the man he'd waited for years to grow up, his dream man, his mate. He was taken by surprise when he felt a pair of hands unzipping his pants, since Ben's hands were wrapped around his waist. He pulled himself away to look.

"Just helping," Thomas said, grinning.

Dillon went back to devouring Ben. This could be the last time he held his mate, a bittersweet goodbye to the man who held his heart and could easily crush him. If Thomas or Ben's wolf refused him, he would end his life. Without a mate he was nothing. There was no reason to go on. Both halves of him were resolved to that path.

"No." Ben jerked back. Only Dillon's hands prevented him from falling on his ass. "You can't do that!"

"Calm yourself," Dillon stroked Ben's bare skin with long soothing touches. "What's wrong?"

"I could hear your thoughts."

Thomas gasped behind Ben. "Fuck, you *are* mates."

Only alphas or mates could read another wolf's thoughts. There was no way Ben was an alpha.

He felt Thomas's hands brush his as they tried to calm the hyperventilating wolf.

"What were you thinking?" Thomas asked. Concern filled his eyes as he took in Ben's pallor.

"If this doesn't work and our wolves reject him, he'll kill himself," Ben said between panicky gasps.

Thomas nodded. "Makes sense."

Ben rounded on him, fangs bared. "It doesn't make sense," he screamed.

* * * *

Thomas watched with a sense of fatality as his mate came completely unhinged. It looked like he was stuck with the other man. He didn't blame Dillon for wanting to seek death without Ben. He would do the same thing. He'd seen wolves lose their mates and try to continue on. They lived a shadowy half-life and lingered for years in a perpetual cloud of despair. Better to end it right away than to exist as a ghost.

There was no way he was going to lose his mate after taking so long to find him, and if it took accepting another wolf to keep him, they would find a way. Despite wanting Thomas's mate, Dillon seemed like a decent guy who wanted what was best for Ben. He couldn't stay angry with the man, it wasn't his fault Ben needed more than one of them.

If anything he felt compassion for the other wolf as Dillon watched all his dreams dissolve. Compassion squeezed Thomas's heart.

"Stay with us, Dillon. I don't want to lose my mate and I have feeling if you were gone Ben wouldn't survive."

"I don't need your pity," Dillon snarled, his wolf teeth flashing.

Thomas punched him in the nose. It made a satisfying crunch as the other man fell down.

"Thomas!" Ben turned a shocked expression towards him.

"I was trying to knock some sense into him," he said innocently. Compassion only got you so far; sometimes it was better to fight it out.

Dillon came back to his feet with a

growl. Ben stepped in his way. Using his supernatural reflexes the other wolf pulled his punch in time. "Careful, sweetie, I almost hit you."

"I'd rather you hit me than you die." Thomas could hear the exasperation and pain in Ben's voice.

"Let's get back on track. Dillon, strip." It amused him to see the other werewolf glare at him before removing the rest of his clothing. Dillon wiped the blood off his face with his shirt before stripping off his boxers with a defiant glare. Thomas could see the other wolf's nose was already healed and back into position. The man was strong even for a shifter. Thomas had barely escaped his attack before. If it came down to the two of them fighting he wasn't entirely convinced he would win. Admiring the other man's chest, it only took a quick look down to feel inadequate.

The man was fucking huge. He was glad Ben told him he'd never been intimate with Dillon before. He wasn't sure he wanted to be in sexual competition with someone this big. However, Ben was right. They would be together for a long time and his body hardened at the thought of having that big monster inside him. He'd never been a size queen before but he might change his mind with a little practice and a lot of access to that big cock.

"I hope you plan on using a lot of lube." Ben snickered.

"I've never had any complaints."

"I bet." Ben sounded dazed.

"You never saw him naked when you shifted?"

It wasn't as if wolves had a taboo about nudity. Hell, on the full moon it was surprising to see them wearing any clothes at all.

"I didn't want to embarrass him by staring. I made sure I changed in a different area."

Dillon laughed. "I didn't give you the same courtesy darlin'. I stared whenever I got the chance. Remove the clothes, I want at that beautiful body."

He didn't know if Dillon was ignoring him on purpose or was just focused on Ben, but he stepped aside so the other man could touch his mate.

Thomas waited for his wolf to growl at the sight of another touching what was his.

And waited.

Nothing.

Huh.

Dillon looked over at him. "Are you

going to attack?"

Thomas shook his head. "So far, so good."

Dillon's shoulders relax a bit as he led Ben to the bed. The other wolf looked back. "Come on, gorgeous, this is at least a three man bed."

His wolf did growl at that. "There is a three man maximum for this bed and don't you forget it." The idea of Dillon touching another man had him seeing red. "A specific three men." He didn't know if the bonding with a second mate would be as strong, but the thought of Dillon touching someone other than Ben or himself made him ill.

Shit, maybe the binding through Ben was stronger than he thought, or that bite he'd received earlier did more than hurt. Only mates were affected by another werekin's bite and Dillon had taken a deep snack on his shoulder.

Thomas smiled. He knew in that moment, everything was going to work out.

Dillon sent a questioning look his way. He pretended not to notice. They could talk about it later. Right now they needed to complete the bonding.

Not wanting to miss out on the mating, he obediently climbed up on the bed, sprawling on the opposite side of Ben so they sandwiched the smaller werewolf between them. He had a feeling this was how they were going to sleep at night. Both of them protecting what was most precious to them.

Ben lay facing Dillon. Thomas knew this was really the bonding for Ben and Dillon, but his wolf refused to be kept out of this moment. For some reason his beast thought if he wasn't here he would miss out on an important part of their life.

Experience taught Thomas never to ignore his wolf.

Dillon kissed Ben. He waited to feel resentment. Waited for his wolf to snap and growl, but all he saw were two beautiful men making love. There was hot passion between them, a flurry of lips against lips with a lot of tongue action, but what brought out Thomas's lust was the gentle hold Dillon had on his mate. The other werewolf's touch was firm but gentle, his grip barely denting the smaller man's delicate skin.

Sliding down his lover's body, Dillon swallowed Ben's cock. Thomas watched his mate touch the other werewolf with a gentle, worshipful touch. As if his greatest dream was coming true. He swallowed back a lump in his throat. Not because he was jealous, but because he was allowed to witness the tender scene.

Pleased with what he was watching, he wanted to join the action. Leaning forward, he licked a line up Ben's back.

CHAPTER FOUR

Dillon moaned around Ben's cock. He'd waited a lifetime to taste his love and it was everything he'd dreamed. Lapping at the hard rod, he was pleased at the whimpers and soft touches he received with every lick. When he felt Ben's balls draw up, he lifted his mouth.

He didn't want Ben coming until he was inside his tight ass. He knew Thomas was doing something behind his mate's back but he didn't want to know what. He concentrated on bringing his lover to the edge and backing off.

"Wait for me, honey. Back or knees?"

"Back. I want to see your eyes."

"Yeah. I wouldn't want you to be confused," he looked away hoping Ben didn't see the flash of pain he knew showed in his eyes. Gentle fingers gripped his chin and turned him back. "What is it, love?" Ben's eyes were filled with tears, not the emotion he was hoping to have his mate feeling when they were about to bond for the first time.

"I'm sorry you can't have a solo mate," Ben sobbed.

Sighing, Dillon brushed his lover's hair back from his face. Glancing over Ben's shoulder he met Thomas's equally troubled expression. Neither of them wanted the small werewolf to be riddled with guilt whenever they got together.

"I know, darling." Dillon took the lube Thomas handed him without looking at the other werewolf. "But I've learned you can't always have everything you want. We'll work it out," he vowed.

At least if they couldn't work things out he knew his little love would have someone to watch over him. Just the feel of Ben beneath him, even once, was worth any amount of heartache.

The feel of a hand stroking his back had him instinctively jerking his head around.

"Easy," Thomas said in a rich voice. Dillon had a feeling the other wolf could make the encyclopedia sound like a dirty bedtime story. "My wolf wants to get a feel for you."

He tried to relax. Really he did, but he didn't know Thomas and his wolf was a cautious soul. He didn't shy away, but he didn't lean into the hand either.

Ben sighed beneath him. "Kiss already. You're making me nervous and my wolf likes you both fine."

Dillon assessed Thomas as a potential

lover. The man wasn't his usual type. His perfect type was lying beneath him waiting for him to kiss another man, but if he met him on the street he would definitely take a second look and maybe a third if he heard him speak.

He was amused to see Thomas looking him over in the same manner. "We're a good-looking pair." Dillon smirked.

"Yes we are," Thomas agreed.

Before he could say any of the other smart-ass comments hovering on his tongue, Thomas grabbed his head between two strong hands and kissed him stupid.

Need rippled up his back, so hot he thought he was on fire. Moaning, he released his hold on Ben and wrapped his arms around Thomas, diving into the kiss and absorbing the other man's sounds.

Impressions and vague thoughts of heat and need filled his head. One thought rose above them all, alerting him to the fact the thoughts weren't all his.

An image of Dillon's cock floated through his mind. *I need to taste that.*

Dillon's head jerked. "I heard you in my mind."

Thomas's eyes went wide. "What did you hear?"

Dillon blushed.

"Well, well," Thomas teased. "You did hear me."

"What were you thinking?" Ben asked.

Thomas nodded indicating that Dillon should answer.

Still blushing Dillon said, "He wanted to taste my dick."

Ben laughed. "He'll have to stand in line. Come here and give me first taste."

Smiling, Dillon climbed up Ben's body until his crotch was even with Ben's mouth. "Taste away, baby. I can't tell you how many nights I dreamed of this moment."

"Don't waste time dreaming when you can be doing. Feed me your cock," Ben said, wrapping his mouth around the tip of Dillon's cock, he sucked it in.

Dillon moaned. He was so sensitive and this was Ben, his dream man. Just watching those cherry lips wrap around his prick was enough to tighten his balls and make him want to shoot. When Ben sucked him halfway and started to moan, he pulled out.

"Mine," Ben growled, his eyes shifted in passion and there was a hint of fang.

"You fanged out, definitely no cock for you. Lift your legs and I'll slick you up. You can suck me off later. There's no way I'm letting you near me with your saber teeth."

Ben snickered. "Fair enough." He turned his head to look at his other mate. "Thomas, would you slick me up?"

Thomas nodded. "Do you mind?" he asked Dillon. "I'd feel better if I knew he was prepared to take you."

Nodding, he slid to one side and let the other man in. With Thomas's hand that close to his body he could feel the heat from the other werewolf. The scent of hot, needy male had him looking down to see a long erect cock between the werewolf's legs. Drops of pre-cum bubbled from the tip, making Dillon's mouth water.

Giving in to instinct he slid down and swiped a tongue to capture the other man's essence.

Flavor exploded across his taste buds.

"Mmmm. More." Need clawed at him with fangs sharper than any wolf. With nothing more in his head than want, Dillon pounced. Thomas hit the floor with Dillon deep-throating his cock.

* * * *

Thomas was going out of his fucking mind. He knew he should be shoving the other man off, but neither his desire nor his wolf cared that they should be concentrating on Ben. Dillon did something with his tongue that made his eyes roll up in his head.

"Fuck." Thomas convulsed in short hip thrusts, which was as much movement allowed by the strong wolf holding him down. With nothing to do but submit, Thomas gave it up, coming down Dillon's throat with a force that drained the essence and all the energy out of him.

A sound above him made him glance up. Ben was leaning over the edge of the bed, watching the pair of them. The smaller wolf's pupils were blown as he made whimpering noises of desire.

"I think our baby is wanting," he whispered to Dillon who was licking his way up Thomas's stomach. It was the last thing he said because the other werekin took his mouth in a no-holds-barred kiss and wiped every other thought out of his mind. His wolf wanted to bare its belly and let this strong man take a bite. He could feel the mating bonds wrapping around them. They would be a true tri-mate. In that moment he knew he would belong to Dillon as much as he did to Ben. His wolf would accept nothing less.

When Dillon lifted off his body, Thomas

almost cried out from the loss. He heard a thump as the big werewolf leaped onto the bed. He didn't worry about the other man harming the redhead. He was one hundred percent certain the other man would cut off his own arm before he hurt Ben.

Soon the sounds coming from the bed had him curious. Groaning he mustered enough strength to sit up and check out the action.

Oh.

Dillon's large body covered the smaller werewolf, his sculptured ass pumping away as he moved in and out of the slim body. Even as he fucked Ben with a feral intensity, his kisses were soft and sweet and Thomas could see the utter joy in his mate's eyes as he looked up at the other man.

Thomas blinked back the sudden watering in his eyes.

They were so fucking beautiful together. Unable to stay away and needing to be part of their lovemaking, Thomas crawled up onto the bed beside the pair. His hands ghosted across them as he yearned to join their mating.

He watched with eager anticipation as Dillon's fangs emerged. Without missing a stroke, the larger wolf impaled Ben's shoulder with his teeth. Not to be outdone, when Dillon released him Ben bit the wolf at the curve between his shoulder and neck, pumping him full of mating endorphins.

Lying beside them with Ben's mating serum in his body from a prior coupling, Thomas felt the click as the two bonded. Relief surged through his body leaving him giddy with joy. The connection between them all rushed through his body. He could feel them both, together and apart. They were a triad.

Dillon was safe now.

CHAPTER FIVE

With Dillon meeting with Anthony about job opportunities and Thomas talking to Silver regarding pack matters, Ben was at loose ends. He'd taken pity on his mate and was now doing the books for the club as well as his personal clients, but he'd finished that a while ago. Hoping he could persuade his men to dance, Ben made his way out to the bar. Smiling at his favorite bartender, he took his seat on a barstool.

"Evening, Dare."

The gorgeous cat shifter gave him a warm smile. Even when he wasn't flirting, the man exuded a joy in life that was irresistible. It was obvious by the people milling around that it was more than the drinks that had them hovering in the drink area.

When he thought no one was looking, Ben saw the cat watching a serious-looking werewolf who gazed everywhere but at the bar.

Ben was dying with curiosity about the pair, but there was a longing in the bartender's eyes that said it was a story too personal to share in a crowded bar.

"What can I get you, pretty man? I'd

offer myself but I hear you have your hands full these days."

He gave the bartender a nod and a smile. "Yeah, I have more than enough on my plate. How about a rum and coke?"

"Coming up." His drink was served with another smile. Ben moved away to let others take his coveted spot. More than a few had their eyes on the bartender rather than their drink choices.

He drifted to the corner of the dance floor to watch all the hot shifters move. He knew Dillon didn't like to dance much but he didn't know about Thomas. It would be great if one of his mates enjoyed dancing, though watching was good too. He tilted his head to the right to understand for a moment how two of the dancers were intertwined. He was pretty sure they would be arrested anywhere else.

As he straightened he felt something cold and sharp press against his throat. Fear frosted his spine as a familiar voice whispered in his ear. "Hello, pretty. I see you lost your man already. That's okay, you have me." Ned's voice was calm and easy, the knife not even mentioned. "You want me don't you, baby? I've been dreaming about you."

Saying no was probably not the best

choice. "I don't think my mate would approve." He hoped that was neutral enough. He didn't think it would be worthwhile to mention he had two mates, neither of whom would appreciate a psychopath cutting his throat. Ned didn't need to know about his love life. The pressing of the knife against his throat told him that wasn't the case.

"Too bad for him. He won't want you when I'm done having my fun."

Shit.

Ben hoped the tentative bond he felt from his mates was enough to get a message to them. As Ned dragged him through the crowds, Ben sent a mental call to his mates for help. He didn't want to involve any of the bar patrons, the psychotic might stab one of them. Ben could tell from the sizzle against his skin that the knife was coated in silver.

Danger. Ned. Help.

He imagined Thomas clearly in his head, and then Dillon.

Ned's body blocked most people from seeing who was in his arms. Before he had any chance to escape or make a plan they were outside in the night. The knife left his throat as he was thrown against the hood of a rusty pickup. He wondered how many other men Ned had kidnapped in the past. It was done too smoothly for it not to be a pattern.

"Now it's my chance to get at that sweet ass."

Without the knife at his throat Ben spun around to confront Ned. Even as his body shook with fear he was resolved to fight. "I'm not going to let you do this."

Ned laughed, his face an ugly mask of need. "How are you going to stop me, pretty boy? We both know I'm the stronger wolf, your mate isn't around, and no one is going to hear you from inside."

Ben knew the other wolf was right. Despair filled him.

"That's right, give in and it'll be easier." Ned gave him a nasty smile. "But go ahead and fight if you want, I'm not against a little rough foreplay."

Nausea churned his stomach. Even if his mates came they wouldn't make it in time. Taking a deep breath, Ben let out his inner beast. Claws slid out of his fingers where nails previously lay. Growling low, he launched himself at Ned.

Pain exploded in his skull as the larger wolf grabbed him around the waist and slammed him down onto the rough gravel.

Ben lay there whimpering as the stronger wolf laughed over him.

"Is there a problem?" A soft tenor asked. The familiar sound of the alpha mate's voice sent terror through Ben's heart. He knew he could survive whatever Ned dished out but he didn't know about the fragile-looking human.

Glancing over, he saw the shadow of a red sports car parked a few feet away. While they were arguing neither of them had heard the car pull up.

Anthony walked out of the shadows.

Ned lit up like a Christmas tree. "Even better. Where are your guards, alpha mate? I didn't think your master let you outside without them," he sneered. "Doesn't matter. I'll fuck you first and then take the pretty one with me."

"I don't think so." Anthony's voice was as calm as if they were discussing the weather. Ben watched in amazement as the slim man picked lint off of his jacket, ignoring the approach of the large werewolf. "I think you're going to get into that disgusting truck of yours and leave town. I can't let you harm a pack member. It would upset my mate."

Lying on the ground, Ben felt a stirring in the air. The little hair he had on his body rose from a sudden incrcase in static clectricity while the smell of ozone filled the air.

He had a very bad feeling about this.

This wasn't going to end well. Struggling to his feet, he was too late to stop the sequence of events unfolding.

Ned let out a roar of laughter. Without warning he lunged at Anthony with his knife. Ben's instinct was to jump in the way but for some reason his feet wouldn't move. He was paralyzed.

His shock couldn't be any stronger than Ned's. Before the vicious werewolf reached Anthony, a bolt of lightning ripped from the sky and fried the bastard where he stood. The werewolf's expression of shock froze on his face. His entire body was completely still as if he were turned into stone.

With one neatly manicured nail, Anthony tapped the body. A crackling sound filled the air and Ned shattered into a million pieces like a cartoon character, but ten times more horrifying. Ben was released from his stasis and rushed over to Anthony, but now he didn't know if he wanted to hug the guy or run away screaming.

Anthony's gold eyes locked onto his. He half expected to see a storm brewing in them but they were calm and clear. "I always tell Silver I can take care of myself."

Ben nodded. "What did you say that other quarter of your heritage was?"

"My grandfather is Zeus."

"Huh." He could see why Silver might not want that advertized. You want your pack to know you can protect them, not scare off your members.

The outer door burst open and his two worried mates rushed to Ben's side.

"Are you all right, sweetheart?" Thomas ran forward followed closely by Dillon.

"We heard you calling but we didn't know where you were. Dare told us you'd gone outside." Dillon's eyes searched him closely, looking for injuries.

Ben watched as his savior walked carefully around the shattered corpse and sauntered up to the alpha standing in the doorway.

"Hello, honey. Sorry I'm late. There was an accident on the way home."

"Where are your bodyguards?" The alpha's tone indicated there would be a reckoning, but Ben knew Anthony would enjoy the process.

Anthony looked around the parking lot. "Hmmm. I guess I must have lost them."

"Get your ass inside, we're going to have a discussion about how dangerous it is to travel without your bodyguards." Silver's voice was low and mean. The alpha looked over at them. "Anything I need to worry about?"

"No sir," Ben said. There was no way he was going to rat Anthony out even if it was to his mate. If the other man wanted his mate to know he'd tell him. He relaxed when the alpha gave him a wink.

"By the way, Dillon, in case my mate didn't tell you, welcome to the pack."

Dillon gave a short bow, tilting his head in deference, holding the pose until the alpha stomped after his mate.

"Fuck they're crazy," he commented.

"Yeah, but they're ours," Ben said, chuckling. "Let's go to bed. I need reassurance from my mates."

Dillon's hands ran up and down Ben's body. "What happened out here?"

He watched as Thomas nudged the ash pile with his foot, the flash of the silver knife shone in the pile. "Is that what I think it is?"

Ben jerked away from Dillon and threw up on the asphalt. The fear of moments ago came back threefold as terror made his hands shake. If Anthony hadn't intervened he might not have survived the evening.

In shaky tones he told his mates what transpired. The three of them stared at the pile of ash with fascination and horror.

"We owe him a debt," Thomas said, swallowing hard.

"Don't worry. With as much trouble as he gets in I'm sure we'll have plenty of opportunities to repay it," Dillon said, dryly.

Ben didn't want to think about the body in the parking lot. It would probably be carried away by the wind anyway. Until five minutes ago he would've sworn what he saw was impossible. Apparently, with the Moon pack nothing was unbelievable. After all, if a pack could have a tri-mate, why couldn't they have a man who was part god, part fae, part witch and all kinds of trouble?

The End

COURTING CALVIN
MOON PACK
BOOK THREE

When Calvin's sister is kidnapped will he be forced to betray a friend to get her back or will the sexy vampire, Alesandro, come to his rescue?

Courting Calvin

MOON PACK, BOOK 3

AMBER KELL

SILVER PUBLISHING
Published by Silver Publishing
Publisher of Erotic Romance

PROLOGUE

"You know what you have to do," the deep voice taunted from the shadows.

Calvin Sanders stood in the empty warehouse. Smells of mold, urine, and excrement filled the air, threatening to gag him while he examined the picture of a stunning blond man who glowed like trapped sunlight.

How had his life come to this?

"I capture him and bring him to you." He squinted against the dark, trying to make out the shape of the speaker but his vision couldn't penetrate the deep blackness of the warehouse. "And what do you do to him?"

"That's none of your business," the stranger growled. "He killed my brother. Bring him to me and I'll see that your sister won't be the next person to die."

"She'll be returned safely?" Calvin asked. Against his will his gaze went back to the picture of his sister tied up, her eyes wide with terror. In front of her was a newspaper, held up so he could see the date. Yesterday. His poor little sister was at the mercy of psychotics since yesterday. Chills shook his frame as he thought of all they could do to a twenty-year old girl in twenty-four hours.

"She'll be released."

He didn't miss the speaker's avoidance of the word 'safely'. Calvin didn't trust the man who wouldn't tell him his name or show his face, but what choice did he have? Leaving his sister in the hands of this obvious psychotic wasn't an option, even if he had a hard time believing this innocent looking man killed anyone. Of course, whether the blond killed anyone or not didn't matter in the scheme of things; he wanted his sister back.

"She's all right?" He couldn't keep the pleading tone out of his voice even as he wished he could take it back.

"You'll have to hope so, won't you?"

"I want to talk to her before I do this."

"You're under the false illusion you have options Mr Sanders. You only have two choices here. You can do as I say and save your sister, or you can choose not to and I can have her body delivered to you in pieces."

Calvin closed his eyes, fighting against the urge to cry. He wasn't a strong person, not like one of those action movie heroes who would've come in guns blazing and killed all the bad guys before saving the girl and possibly the world. He was a woodworker who had tried hard to raise a little girl who lost her parents way too young. Until now he thought he'd done a good job. Until his job became the reason she was kidnapped.

He was never going to take a gig working for paranaturals again.

Fuckers!

They both knew he had no options, but the thought she could already be dead was a sharp pain in his heart. He took a deep breath. "I'll do it."

"I knew we'd come to an agreement," the man said, his voice rich with satisfaction. "Don't take too long to capture him. I don't have much patience and I can't guarantee your sister's safety longer than a week."

Calvin nodded, his stomach churning as he fled the warehouse to the sound of laughter.

CHAPTER ONE

Alesandro leaned over and spoke into the beautiful blond's ear. "Do you think he's single?"

"Maybe. He's not wearing a ring and he did stare at me when we were introduced."

The vampire snorted. "That only means he's not blind."

A low laugh was his companion's response. Al smiled. He liked making Anthony laugh. Over the past few months of building the para-only hotel, they had become good friends. He admired Anthony a great deal; he was a sweet man and a brilliant architect. The meeting tonight was to talk with the woodworker about the design for the vampire suites.

The two of them had made a deal where Al, the master vampire of a small group, would provide consultation in exchange for the occasional use of one of the rooms. Vampires were extremely territorial and this would make a good conciliatory gesture when an important vamp he didn't want to house at the tower came into town.

Watching the luscious man lean over to get a measurement, he had to admit there was more than one benefit to this arrangement.

"Stop drooling. You're going to make the poor boy nervous. Not to mention he might slip in the wet spot," Anthony said with a teasing smile.

"The poor boy's name is Calvin," the carpenter said, turning around and looking at the pair. "And the day I mind being stared at by two gorgeous men is the day they dig a hole and throw me in it, because I'll be dead."

He flashed a smile showing a pair of deep dimples in his tanned cheeks. Warm brown eyes twinkling with amusement watched them both. The man's skin had an olive cast that spoke of some Spanish heritage somewhere in his family tree.

Yummm.

"I guess we're not strong on subtlety," Anthony said. "By the way, thanks for coming after hours. Alesandro here doesn't do well in the sunlight."

"Wow, you really aren't subtle," Alesandro said, shaking his head. "My brazen friend has hung out with too many werewolves lately, but that does beg the question as to whether you'd mind dating a vampire."

Calvin laughed. "I can tell you're the subtle one."

"Nah, I just dazzle them with my smile," Alesandro said, flashing his pearly whites.

The woodworker shook his head and turned back to his measuring, making notes in a small notebook he kept in his front pocket when not scrawling obscure notations inside. Al had snuck a peek earlier but hadn't been able to make out what the different numbers referred to.

"If you do good work I'll have other jobs for you. This is just the first of many projects I have in mind," Anthony said.

"I don't suppose Silver is aware of your *other* projects?" Al asked without much hope. Anthony took great joy in keeping his big, bad mate on his toes.

"Now what fun would that be?" he asked, batting his long eyelashes. "I wouldn't want my mate to become bored."

Calvin laughed again, and Alesandro decided he could get used to the sound.

Even though he knew other things needed his attention, he couldn't stop his eyes from wandering up and down the young, hot woodworker. His body was in complete agreement about the beauty of the view. There wasn't anything about the young man that didn't appeal. From his strong calloused fingers to his wide shoulders and muscled physique, the man was smoking hot. Throw in the pretty dark hair and soulful brown eyes and the entire package was irresistible.

Yumm.

His mind knew he was too old to drool over a hot young stud but his other body parts were unconvinced. His cock in particular was anxious for an introduction.

A wolf howl sounded in the room, startling him from his thoughts.

Anthony gave a sheepish smile and lifted the tiny cell phone out of the holster on his hip.

"Hi, sugarlips," he said into the receiver.

Alesandro snorted. The various pet names the sleek blond gave his huge, buff werewolf mate were a source of constant amusement, but it was the love in Silver's eyes when he looked at Anthony that kept the mocking at a minimum. It was hard to taunt someone who didn't give a crap. Common knowledge around the para community was that Silver would do anything for his beautiful mate as long as his safety wasn't an issue.

A veritable fleet of bodyguards surrounded the man at all times, keeping him safe from cranky hotel guests and vicious paper cuts, because those were the only dangers Alesandro ever saw attacking the stunning blond.

"Al, I've got to get home to Silver, he's having a minor meltdown about the time. Do you think you can show Calvin the other things we discussed, especially the bar?" The vampire wasn't fooled. His friend was purposely leaving him alone with his current obsession.

Anthony smelled of lust after talking to his mate. Alesandro's fangs slid down a fraction at the alluring scent. With force of will he pulled his teeth back into his gums before responding. Ruining the relationship between his vampire clan and the wolves, and endangering his own life, weren't in his plans for the evening. He knew that, despite Anthony's friendliness, the man's bodyguards would rip out Al's throat if he so much as sniffed the man inappropriately.

"Absolutely. I'd be happy to." Images of all the things he could show the young man flashed through his brain like a high definition porno.

"Thanks, you're a dear." Anthony placed a soft kiss on his cheek and dashed out the door with a breezy wave goodbye to Calvin. Alesandro watched with amusement as the blond ignored the two werewolves who detached themselves from the wall and followed him out. It was as if he was so used to people following him that he didn't even see them anymore.

"Does he always have bodyguards?" Calvin asked coming up to the vampire's side as they watched Anthony leave. That was one man who was a good view coming and going.

He nodded. "I'm sure you were warned when you came to work for Anthony that Silver is very protective."

Calvin snorted. "You mean, when the scary as fuck werewolf told me if I touched his man he would 'snap my neck like a toothpick and throw me in the meadow for the wolves to eat'? Nothing says welcome to the company quite like a death threat."

Alesandro laughed. "To answer your question, yes, Anthony always has bodyguards. It's not uncommon for one werekin pack to kidnap important members from another pack to get territory concessions." He tilted his head towards Anthony's exit. "And it isn't exactly a secret that Silver would do anything for his mate. He may be the strongest wolf in North America but that little blond is his biggest weakness."

Calvin gave him a strange look that Alesandro couldn't interpret.

* * * *

Alone with the vamp, Cal's nerves trembled. He didn't mind Anthony watching him because he could feel it was admiring, not offensive, but the vampire looked at him like he was the man's next lunch.

With a vampire that was a real possibility.

"Relax, handsome." Alesandro's voice was smoky, like good jazz. It made Cal want to wrap himself in the other man's essence. Only the knowledge he was soon to betray the man's friend kept him from jumping the handsome vamp.

Calvin snuck another look at the vampire and felt his body go hard all over. Fuck, he could almost come from the look in those gorgeous green eyes alone. Alesandro had that whole sexy vampire thing going, with short black hair lying shiny and smooth across his well-shaped head, large mesmerizing green eyes, and a tall, slim body that made everything in Calvin ache. However, it was the power pouring off the other man and engulfing him with pulsing desire that made him want to slam Alesandro against the wall and grind against the vampire until they both came. Images of different sexual positions possible in an enclosed area kept him hard and aching as he measured the space and calculated time for his projects. He hid his erection by turning his back to the other man and sketching rough estimates in his notebook. He wondered briefly if vampires could really read minds.

A low chuckle drew his attention back to Alesandro's face.

"Is there something you're trying to hide from me?" The vampire pinned him with a cool look. Calvin's dick got harder beneath those stunning green eyes even as relief filled him. If the vampire couldn't read his mind then Calvin wouldn't have to worry about blocking his thoughts. He was still trying to figure how to grab the blond from his cadre of bodyguards, and the clock was ticking.

A little diversion was called for.

"I'm sure there's all kinds of things I'm trying to hide from you," he confessed. "Right now it's the condition of my cock."

Leaning over, Calvin took a final measurement. If he wiggled a little more than necessary to distract the vamp, neither of them mentioned it. The heat flaring in Alesandro's eyes when he glanced back should've set off the newly installed smoke detectors.

"Now that I know what Anthony is looking for, I can get the rest of these started tomorrow and finished by the end of next week. I'll build up the bed frames so that the vampire beds will fully recess below and lock from the inside. I'll also adjust them to fit a feathertop mattress so vampires can have comfort as well as safety. Anyone looking in the room will see an empty raised bed unless, of course, the vampire brings a human companion, in which case they can sleep in the upper bed without crushing the one below. The bed skirt will hide the lower compartment so it won't be in view and Anthony mentioned only security-cleared maids will have access to the beds. The custom fireplace for the lobby will take a few weeks to carve and the design he wants on the stairway could take up to a month. Do you think he'll have a problem with that?"

Alessandro shrugged. "I'll ask him tomorrow. What about the bar?"

Calvin straightened from his position crouched on the floor. "What about the bar?"

"Anthony wants wolves carved along the edge of the bar to represent his lover's pack."

"Cool. I can do wolves. In fact if you get me pictures I can even make it look like members of the pack." Calvin first dreamed of being an artist before responsibility demanded he learn his grandfather's woodworking skills. When the old man died he'd left Calvin alone with his younger sister and a rich woodcarving heritage. Unfortunately it was the only thing they inherited besides a small house and a set of kick ass carving tools. He pushed to the back of his mind the fact he wouldn't be there to do the project, no matter how enticing. When he betrayed Anthony he was certain the pack alpha would investigate very quickly. Once Silver found out that Calvin betrayed his mate, his chances of staying alive weren't very good.

If only he could stay and work with Anthony. The thought of betraying the man who wanted to make a place for all para-kind ate at his gut. Not only was it a good project, but the guy was really nice. The whole crew was. From the first day, well, after the alpha death threat, everyone on staff treated him like he was one of the pack instead of an outside guy doing a little work. Unfortunately, with his sister's life on the line, blood would win over friendship every time. He couldn't afford to enjoy being one of the group, not when his sister could be going through torture while he enjoyed the job opportunity of a lifetime. He was pulled out of his grim thoughts by the vampire's next words.

"Come, I'll take you to the bar so you can get an idea of the scope of the work."

Alesandro led him to the stairs, opening the door for Calvin to go through first. Other than a raised brow, the carpenter didn't ask why they weren't using the elevator. He knew vampires didn't like enclosed spaces, except when they slept. He'd done his research before he accepted the job. Anthony was also offering windowless bedrooms for those who wanted a more airy environment, since there was always an exception to the rule. The man thought of everything.

The two of them walked down the stairs without comment. He had no idea what Alesandro was thinking, but he did admire the view as they made their way down two flights to the main lobby.

They came out into a marbled hall that brought a new level to the word luxurious. Designed to appeal to the paranatural world, the entry was a combination of sinful luxury and interesting details made to appeal to different factions. A water feature started with a lion at one end of the lobby pouring water out of its mouth then flowing down a long, shallow waterway to the east wall of the lobby and ending in a shallow pool with a small fountain decorated with mermaids and fairies. Little flashes of gold alerted guests to the tiny fishes swimming within. Elaborate blown glass lights were all set on low as most paras either had enhanced night vision or were sensitive to bright lights. Even the walls had special paint designed to have an extra layer of color to those with spectral vision. Tucked amongst the potted plants and beautiful fixtures were small statues of wolves, lions, bears, and other fantastical forms so that all felt welcome.

"He's made something special here," Calvin said coming to stand beside Alesandro. "I'm not a para and even I can feel the care given to this place; the details are incredible." They tilted their heads to look at the vaulted ceiling where the moon glowed softly through specially coated windows. In the full light of day a vampire could walk safely through the lobby.

Alesandro nodded. "It's something special all right, and you're here to make sure it's even more special. Come on, the bar is this way."

He led the way through an arched doorway decorated with nymphs.

Calvin barely had time to admire the bar's beautiful wooden top before a long firm body was at his back pressing him against the hard surface.

"You are such a beautiful man," Alesandro whispered in his ear. Soft lips brushed against the fine hairs on Calvin's skin sending shivers down his spine.

Cal's back arched from the sensation. When did the vampire get so close?

"Um. Thank you," he glanced down at the bar, anxious to change the subject, anything to distract the hot man behind him. Although he longed for Alesandro with a gnawing ache in his gut, he couldn't get involved with the man. They had no future and he had enough baggage right now to open a luggage store.

"I don't think I've ever seen such a large piece of wood before."

"I've got some wood for you right here," the vampire said rubbing his hard prick against Cal's ass.

So much for distraction. He tried again. "It looks like one piece."

Sighing, Alesandro stepped back. "It was donated by a dying dryad. Her tree was rotting from some sort of disease so she allowed them to cut it down and bring the tree here."

"Didn't that kill her?"

The vampire leaned his entire body

against Calvin's, rubbing their cheeks together. The rough scrape of Alesandro's whiskers sent another shiver through the carpenter. His dick was so hard he could drill a hole through the bar. Who needed tools?

"Anthony felt it would be murder to take the dryad's tree, and give the hotel a bad aura, so he hired a witch to transfer her to a healthy young oak before cutting this one down."

Amazing. Touching the wood, Calvin thought he could almost hear the memories of the forest vibrating beneath his fingertips.

Alesandro's hands gripped Calvin's hips, pulling him into the vee of the man's thighs. One hand released him and stroked the wood next to Calvin's fingers, evoking images of other things he could be stroking. "You can almost feel the love the dryad had for this tree. I think Anthony made the right decision, even if it did add to the cost. Did the witch charge him a lot?" He couldn't imagine anyone taking advantage of the blond, not with his growly protector, but there were a lot of fools in the world.

He felt Alesandro shrug. "She asked for a few nights here in exchange. It was the cost of getting the tree cut down, shaped, and installed that was so pricey. I think, in the end, the bar will add a lot to the hotel. I can feel its calming magic as soon as I enter the bar. I believe Anthony was thinking of his mate when he installed it. A bit of forest magic in the middle of the city will help calm the wolves."

"That's so sweet." To go to all that trouble for his mate raised Calvin's estimation of Anthony and dug the guilt in deeper. Anyone who went to that much trouble wasn't a stone cold killer.

"I can show you sweet."

Alesandro spun him around and pressed him once more against the bar. The vampire had a good two inches and twenty pounds of muscle on him and the man used it to good effect as he kissed every thought right out of Calvin's head.

A hard grip held his hips, preventing him from rubbing against the glorious man who kissed like a god. Desire building, Calvin whimpered as the vampire held him just far enough away he could feel the hard cock brushing against his, but not close enough he could do anything about it.

Calvin tore his mouth free. "Rub me, suck me, or fuck me, I don't care, but do *something*," he growled at the sexy vampire.

"I am doing something." Alesandro smirked before diving in for another kiss.

Maybe he could break off a piece of the

bar and impale the bastard with it. Just when he was considering methods of killing the other man he got his wish. Deft hands unfastened his button fly denims, releasing him from clothing confinement.

"No underwear," Alesandro said, smiling. "So much easier to consume you, my dear."

"No fangs," Calvin warned as the beautiful vamp sank to his knees in a liquid, graceful movement hotter than any wet dream. Every fantasy he'd ever had was wrapped up in the gorgeous stud eyeing his cock like it was the best kind of candy. Although he'd never considered vampires as potential lovers before, the pure beauty of the man made him more than willing to at least give this one a try.

"No fangs," Alesandro agreed. "Besides, I don't know you well enough to bite you."

He wondered how well a vampire needed to know its victim. Before he could ask, the vampire swallowed him whole, sucking every thought out of his mind and through his cock like a straw.

"God damn, fuck," Calvin cursed, bucking his hips. Once again, those damn hands gripped his hips, preventing further movement and sending burning heat through his body.

One day soon, he was going to be the one pinning down the gorgeous vamp and fucking that fine ass. He screamed, his brain melting as he pulsed out his release in an embarrassingly short time. The smell of sex filled the air.

Alesandro rose gracefully to his feet, licking his lips.

Calvin wanted to lick them for him but worried it was too intimate for what was essentially a one-time fuck. He couldn't risk getting close to Alesandro, especially since Anthony was his friend. A friend he was going to have to betray to get his sister back.

"Give me a moment and I'll help you out with this," Calvin said, pressing his palm against the hard column bulging Alesandro's tailored pants. His breath came in short gasps as he tried to calm his pounding heart. That was the hardest he'd come in a long time.

"Turn around and bend over, beautiful, and I'll take care of it myself."

Calvin swallowed nervously. "It's been a while." He didn't want to deny the vamp, but it had been a few years since he last bottomed.

"Don't worry, I'll be gentle."

For some reason, Calvin believed him. As he turned around, Calvin could feel by the man's gentle touch that Alesandro had no interest in causing him pain. Divested of the rest of his clothing in quick, easy movements, Calvin gave a nervous glance at the doorway.

"No one will come in, I've ensured our privacy." Alesandro's low soothing voice calmed his fears even as the man's presence enflamed his desire.

"Lean over, beautiful." The vampire's hand pushed him carefully over the bar. Calvin gave in to the pressure, lifting his ass to angle his body for ease of entry.

A loud groan sounded behind him.

"Come and get me, stud," Calvin teased, looking over his shoulder. If he kept it light-hearted maybe they could end this encounter with nice memories on both sides. Soon Alesandro would have enough bad thoughts about him.

"Oh, don't worry. I will." The look in the vampire's gaze told Calvin he was everything the vampire wanted and aimed to have.

Turning back around, Calvin lifted his hips higher to entice his lover.

* * * *

Alesandro almost swallowed his tongue.

It took all of his concentration to keep the deterrent spell on the bar entrance going as he admired the fine ass before him.

Despite all his centuries of life and innumerable sexual encounters, this was the first time Al felt a compulsion to claim someone as his own. It was difficult to keep his promise not to bite his lover when all he could think of was how the sweet man would taste.

His fangs dropped despite his best efforts to keep them recessed in his gums. He didn't just want to fuck Calvin, he needed to. More than he needed blood, he needed to be inside the gorgeous carpenter who made works of beauty with his hands and looked at him like he was one of the wonders of the world. Something about those soulful brown eyes filled with light and desire spun Alesandro's world on its axis and, like a divining rod to water, his cock led the way to the tight ass presented before him.

Pulling a packet of lube out of his pocket, he quickly ripped off his clothing, not caring if he destroyed his expensive suit in the process.

Nothing was keeping him from Calvin. Luckily, vampires didn't need condoms; they couldn't spread disease and he'd never been gladder of that fact than at that moment.

Tearing the lube open, he slathered it liberally on the fingers of his left hand and used the remaining lube on his prick. He took the time to loosen up his lover with one finger, then two, and eventually three. Despite the shaking of his own body, he wouldn't rush this moment for anything in the world. If he hurt the man trustingly offering up his body, he would never forgive himself.

Once he was satisfied Calvin was loose enough, he gave in to the soft whimpering, lined himself up, and pressed inside.

They both moaned at the contact.

So good. So fine. So hot and silky inside.

For a moment, Alesandro stilled, sunk to the hilt inside his lover, knowing he would never have this again. Never have another first time with the gorgeous man beneath him.

"If you don't move I'm going to beat you to death with the first thing I can find," Calvin said in a strained voice.

Chuckling Alesandro placed a gentle kiss between the man's thickly muscled shoulders. "I didn't want to hurt you, sugar."

"Fuck... me... now," was the grunted response as Calvin shoved back against

Alesandro, clenching his ass and sucking the will out of the vampire through his prick.

"Fuck."

Unable to resist the siren call of his lover's ass, Alesandro held on tight and pumped in and out with controlled power, careful of using his vampire strength. He wanted this man to remember only good things about this encounter. Otherwise he might not be willing to do it again. Reaching around, he gripped Calvin's quickly hardening cock, pumping him as his hips drilled in and out of that fine, muscled body. He always liked a man who kept in shape, but the human beneath him had muscles honed by hard work, not a gym bunny who spent all his time staring at the mirror while flexing his muscles. This was a real man, and it had been so long since he'd had one of those. His gums tingled but he ruthlessly kept his fangs from bursting through; resisting the urge to bite into the warm body beneath his and take the hot blood he could smell beneath the sweat and sex was one of the hardest things he'd ever done.

Alesandro pumped his hips harder. He needed to end this before he lost all his control and broke the vow he'd made.

"Come. I've got you."

As if he was just waiting for the words,

Calvin exploded, jerking fluid all over the bar. At the smell of the human's release Alesandro came, filling the man's ass in one glorious burst. The combined smell of their scents had him battling his fangs again. He itched to taste the man beneath him but he hadn't missed the cautious looks the human sent him. If he broke trust with the gorgeous man he would most likely not get another shot.

Luckily, after centuries of living, waiting was something he did very well.

Alesandro grabbed a rag from the bar, wiped them both down, and dressed, watching in silence as Calvin slid on his own clothing. The other man's quiet was unnerving after the moans and cries from moments ago.

Did he regret their lovemaking? Calvin found another cloth and wiped down the bar, careful to get every drop.

"I'd love to take you out some time. Or even stay in," Al said cautiously. He slid one cool finger down the side of Cal's face, needing the physical contact as he felt the human already withdrawing. He wasn't one to beg, but he would definitely pursue if the gorgeous woodworker thought to run.

* * * *

Calvin looked at the sincere expression in the vampire's eyes and felt like crap. This handsome man truly wanted him. When was the last time a man made him feel special? He couldn't remember, maybe never.

At Alesandro's touch, desire racked Calvin's body. It felt like a line of fire went from his cheek to his balls. He swallowed audibly, his dry throat clicking like he was in the Sahara.

"I don't date my boss."

That was a reasonable excuse, wasn't it?

"Excellent. Anthony is your boss, I'm more of a consultant. And I can guarantee you won't be dating Anthony."

Before Cal could voice his opinion on dating consultants, Alesandro's lips covered his and all thoughts flew out of his brain. Base needs filled his mind, carnal images of heat and naked flesh. How he wanted this man, vamp, whatever.

When he was finally released he handed his business card over to the vamp in a daze. "My personal number is on the back."

Without another word he all but raced for the door, not daring to look back. It was a mistake. It was all a horrible mistake, but he was damned if he could resist. Calvin rationalized that he should date the vampire now, because after Silver found out he kidnapped Anthony he wouldn't be alive to enjoy it later.

CHAPTER TWO

Calvin left the hotel like the hounds of hell were nipping at his heels. He didn't even remember the drive home as he pulled into his garage, surprised to discover he'd already reached his house.

The phone started ringing as soon as he entered. Anxiety gripped him when he saw the name on caller ID read 'blocked'. Had they been watching him this entire time? The thought they might have seen him with Alesandro made his stomach churn. With shaking hands he pressed the connect button.

"Hello."

"When are you going to deliver Anthony?" The familiar voice came across the line, chilling like winter frost.

"I don't know. They have him surrounded with bodyguards at all times."

"Then get rid of the guards. Drug them, shoot them, I don't care. You have until Friday to deliver him or your sister is dead. Check your mail."

The connection ended.

Fuck.

Calvin tore open his door and ran out of

the house to the mailbox at the end of his drive. It took him a few tries to pull it open, terror making his grip weak. Finally he twisted it open and pulled out his mail. He didn't look at the contents as he slammed the box closed and ran back to his house. He felt exposed as he looked up and down the street trying to spot the man. They were watching, he knew that now. Otherwise, how would they know the moment he got home?

It wasn't until the safety of the door was at his back that he dared to look at the mail in his hand.

Bill. Bill. Ad. White envelope with no address.

The rest fell from his nerveless fingers.

This was it.

From the stiffness of the envelope he could tell it was photos, but what kind? Would they be of his sister injured, tortured… dead?

With his heart racing with fear, he ripped open the envelope with too much force. A picture flew out of his hand and slid across the wooden floor. Falling to his knees, Calvin grabbed the photo. His sister looked up at him with a brand new bruise spread across one cheek. Written on the white part of the photo in black permanent marker were the words:

This is just the beginning

The things a group of thugs could do to a young girl froze his soul. He barely made it to the toilet before everything came back up. Several minutes of retching passed before there was nothing left but dry heaves.

Any doubt the man was bluffing flew out of his head. Tears slid from his eyes as he sobbed in the solitary confines of his bathroom. How could he give Anthony to these psychopaths knowing they would kill him? How could he trade one life for another? Swallowing back the lump in his throat, he tore off some toilet paper and wiped up his tears.

Quickly brushing his teeth, he stared at the mirror. Even if he saved his sister he didn't know if he could ever look himself in the mirror again. His choices weren't easy because no matter how much he liked Anthony and felt bad about betraying Alesandro, there was no way he wasn't going to try and save the little girl he'd loved his entire life.

Their parents had died in a car wreck when they were young and they were sent to live with their grandfather. With hands crippled by arthritis, the older man lived on his disability checks, the government aid he received barely enough to live off of by himself. Unable and unwilling to turn away two kids in need, he passed on the few bits of knowledge he could. Through trial and error the older man taught his grandson all of his woodworking skills so that if something happened he could take care of his sister. Two years later, when their grandfather died of a heart attack, seventeen-year old Calvin took responsibility for his twelve-year old sister. He didn't regret his choices, but he would regret not trying to save her. Even now, at twenty, in his eyes she was still the little girl who came running to her big brother for comfort when she skinned her knee.

    The phone rang again. He knew who it was. Not bothering to check caller id, he pressed the connect button and screamed into the receiver. "I got the photo you bastard."

    Silence came over the line.

    "I didn't send you any pictures, baby. Why don't you tell me what the hell is going on?"

    Calvin hung up.

    Shit.

    Alesandro.

    Why didn't he check the caller ID? He always checked the caller ID.

    The phone rang again.

    Calvin looked at it as though it was a

viper about to strike. Caller ID flashed 'blocked'. Worried it could be the man from the warehouse he reluctantly picked it up again.

"You have two seconds to tell me what the devil is going on or I'm going to become very angry," Alesandro hissed over the line.

Fuck.

"Alesandro, I can't deal with you right now. I've got my own problems." Betrayal... death... the usual.

"Your problems are my problems, sugar. Stay there, I'll be right over."

"No." Calvin sighed as listened to empty air, then the dial tone. "I wonder if it's true that vampires have to be invited in."

"Nope," Alesandro said.

Calvin jumped. "Shit, you scared the crap out of me."

Alesandro's green eyes examined him intently. "No, someone else already did that."

Before he could come up with an excuse for his behavior two strong arms wrapped around him in a comforting embrace. For just a moment he closed his eyes and pretended he was in the arms of someone who cared. Sighing, he sank into the vampire's hug, letting those big shoulders carry his burden, if only for a little while.

"They have my sister," he confessed against the vampire's shoulder as tears welled in his eyes once more. He was never going see his sister again. For a moment he didn't think the vampire heard him, but then those strong arms tightened.

"What do they want?" No wasting time on shock or horror, just a simple request for information.

"Anthony," Calvin choked out, tears filling his eyes. "They want Anthony."

"Shh. Don't cry, sugar." Alesandro's hands stroked his back in long, soothing caresses like he was someone precious. It was a beautiful illusion, but just an illusion nonetheless. There was no way the vampire wasn't going to tell Anthony someone was out to capture him. Calvin would've told if the shoe were on the other foot. "We'll figure something out."

"They're going to kill her." Calvin picked up the picture from the floor and handed it over. "They've had her for a week. Who knows what they've done to her so far?" His hand shook so much the vampire took the picture away from him to get a better look.

"This her?" Alesandro's green eyes searched his.

Calvin nodded.

"She's almost as pretty as you."

"Cindy's much prettier than me," Calvin said, blinking back more tears. Shit, he cried more than a girl. Cindy would kick him in the balls for acting like a baby. Hell, if the situation were reversed she'd probably be looking for grenades and make the kidnapping bastard afraid of the dark.

"Tomorrow, after we rest, we'll go to the pack and tell them what's going on. Silver will know how to get her returned. Until then, you need to know I will always be there for you, baby. You are mine."

A flicker of flame glowed in the vampire's eyes. It should've made him run in fear, or at the very least, unsettled him. Instead, the possessiveness gave him a warm feeling that spread throughout his body. It felt good to let go of his control and give his burden to someone else. Even if the someone else was going to turn him over to the werewolves.

"Now I'm going to make you mine," Alesandro growled.

Buttons flew as the vampire ripped off Calvin's shirt, giving in to passion and impatience. How had it happened within a day, this burning need for a man who wasn't even human? Giving in to instinct, he bit Alesandro on the neck.

Alesandro went wild. He lifted Calvin into the air with the strength of his powerful arms.

"Hold onto me," the vampire demanded.

Instinctively, Cal wrapped his long legs around Alesandro's waist and his arms around the vampire's neck. However, there weren't enough forces in the universe to stop his body from humping against the other man's hard abs as if his life depended on it.

The world blurred for a moment and then he was airborne. Calvin bounced on his bed of unmade cotton sheets and pillow-topped comfort.

Before he could make any smartass comment about Alesandro not knowing his own strength, the vampire's hot mouth consumed him. How a cold vampire could have such burning lips, he didn't know, but for the first time he understood the phrase 'being swept away in the heat of passion'; something he'd scoffed at before when his friends cried on his shoulder after a regrettable night.

Maybe he'd been dating the wrong guys.

The feel of smooth fingers sliding against his skin was almost Calvin's undoing.

He lifted his hips to increase contact only to be pinned down by strong hands. Again.

"Easy, gorgeous. I'm right here." Long, drugging caresses swept up and down his sides. Calvin moaned at the sensation.

Alessandro placed kisses across Cal's body as he touched every inch of his skin.

When did he lose all his clothes? His mind shut down as the vampire did decadent things with his mouth and hands. Buck naked, he lay on the soft comforter and let the vampire have his way as worries and pressure melted away beneath Alesandro's skilled touches.

"Ohh." A nip on the curve of his hip made his back bow with pleasure. His ass clenched and he felt empty. Calvin needed to be filled more than he needed his next breath.

"Please, baby, please. Fuck me."

"Baby?" The vampire stopped what he was doing to laugh. "I'm several hundred years older than you. I'm hardly a baby."

Cal forced his eyes open. "If you don't fuck me soon I'm going to stab you through the heart and then you won't care what I call you."

Alesandro made a tsking sound and shook his head. "We need to talk about your violent tendencies. Threatening your lover is never a good plan. Not when he can hold you down with one hand and lift a car with the other."

Cal laughed. "I don't see any cars here so I'll have to take your word for that."

"You do that." Alesandro rubbed noses with Cal, like a big cat.

Kisses were something Cal did for his lovers to excite them and get them ready for the main event. Alesandro's kisses were an entirely different experience. He was almost positive he could come just from one of the vampire's kisses alone. Desire raced through him like a wildfire at the brief contact.

"Kiss me," he whispered against the vampire's lips, desperate to feel that hot mouth against his once again. This might be the last time he felt the delicious man against him and he wanted to make the most out of the experience. Damn, Alesandro was fine.

With a wide smile the vampire kissed Cal's neck. "Let me show you what a man who doesn't need to breathe can do."

Cal whimpered as the vampire meandered down his body, giving him gentle love bites as he travelled down his chest, his stomach, and slowly reached his destination. The hard member rose to greet Alesandro's mouth as if it, too, yearned for his attention. In one swallow the vampire took him to the root, sending ripples of sensation echoing up his spine.

"Shit," he screamed. Wet heat surrounded his cock and the suction made his eyes roll back into his head. Hell, once with a vamp... he may never be suited to dating mortal men again. "You have the mouth of a god," he moaned, reaching down to stroke the silky head sliding up and down his cock. Familiar tension built up along his spine. "I'm going to come."

"No, you will not." The vampire tugged on Cal's balls. "You will wait for me."

In the darkened room he heard the shushed sound of drawer opening, the snick of a cap letting him know Alesandro had found his supplies. Slick fingers slid inside his body; one, then two, and by the third he was begging in soft, whimpering tones.

"Please, please, please," he chanted.

"Shhh, I'll give you everything you need, my gorgeous man."

* * * *

Alesandro could see perfectly in the dark. Watching the beautiful creature thrashing below him excited him more than any encounter he could remember. Something about the slim young carpenter with tough muscles and a torn heart pulled at him like a beacon.

He could be the one.

Unable to stand the separation any longer, Alesandro slid into the tight, warm hole of his lover, letting out a groan at the sensation.

All lovers before Calvin faded out of existence. Right here and now there were only the two of them in the entire world, wrapped in a cocoon of heat, darkness, and passion.

He reached down and took Calvin's hard prick in his hand, pumping it in counterpoint to each thrust. The two men groaned together. Damn he felt good.

"Harder, baby, harder," Calvin said in between soft moans.

"You're a demanding thing, aren't you?"

"Shut up and fuck me like you mean it."

Well, he couldn't let that challenge pass now, could he? After all, he always meant it. With renewed vigor Alesandro pounded into the young human until he felt Calvin's release pulsing in his hand. Unable to stop himself, Alesandro pressed his body all along his handsome lover's and bit into the juncture between Calvin's shoulder and neck. The human beneath him gave a strangled shout before hardening again. That was one advantage to a vampire bite they didn't advertise. If more humans knew vampire bites were the ultimate aphrodisiac they would be lining up around the block to get bitten. However, the bite was sweeter if the vampire had an emotional connection to the person they bit. Biting strangers was all right in a pinch, but it was so much better to bite a lover during orgasm than a bored club baby who just wanted to get off.

Sweet. Calvin tasted liked warmed honey with a little bit of spice, a rich cacophony of flavors. The young woodworker was a complex meal. One Alesandro would love to sample a great deal more in the future. Maybe forever.

He continued to suck until Calvin found his second release. Then he carefully disengaged his fangs, licking the spot to close the wound and heal the marks left behind. One day soon he would leave behind a scar to mark this human as his own, but not today. Today his beautiful man had too many worries, and when he marked Calvin forever he wanted to be the only thing on his lover's mind.

"Fuck, you're amazing," Calvin said in a dazed voice. "If I knew it was this good I would've had a vamp in my bed years ago."

Alesandro growled, the sound low and mean in the stillness of the house. "You don't need any other vampires, pretty man. All you need is me."

A cold chill filled his chest as he realized he meant that. He didn't like the idea of the gorgeous, dark-haired man below him seeking others out, in any capacity.

He was so screwed.

For the first time in his long life Alesandro was in love, and the thought of a delicate mortal holding his heart in such fragile, easily broken hands scared the usually unflappable vamp.

Alesandro licked his lips savoring the taste of his lover. The downside was, after biting the younger man he now knew his secrets.

"You can't kidnap Anthony," he said into the stillness of the room. "I'll call a council meeting. We'll find a way to save your sister." Alesandro tried to infuse as much confidence into the words as he could, but Silver was more likely to kill the gorgeous carpenter than help him.

CHAPTER THREE

They were all crowded around the boardroom: Anthony, vampires, wolves, and one single human. Cal felt shame flush his cheeks as Anthony watched him with concern instead of the disdain he knew he deserved. It was strange that the most sympathetic person in the room was the one he'd planned to betray. Mikel and Darian, vampires in Alesandro's group, made no attempt to hide their disgust. They alternated between glaring at him or Alesandro, and the look from Silver should've killed him on the spot.

He wasn't seeking disapproval from the werewolf, but it made him feel a little less guilty than the unflagging understanding he received from the slim blond.

Calvin was convinced it was only the gentle restraint of one fine-boned hand on his shoulder that prevented the Moon pack alpha from leaping over the table and ripping out his throat.

"Tell us again about this person and how he got your sister. Why you?" Anthony asked.

"And why we should care," another wolf spoke up. Cal vaguely identified the tall dark-haired man as Dillon, one of the landscape designers. The werewolf looked at him with about as much favor as the pack alpha, Silver, did. He wasn't sure how everyone fit in the hierarchy, but he knew he was currently the least favorite person in the room.

Taking a deep breath he told his story. "My parents died when we were young, it's just me and my sister Cindy. She's living with me while she goes to college to save money.

"What's she studying?" Anthony asked.

"What the fuck do we care what she's studying?" Silver growled, his grey eyes dark with anger. "I want to know why this asshole wants to kidnap my mate and why the hell I shouldn't just rip out his throat."

"Because then we won't know who sent him, will we?" Anthony said in such a reasonable tone it was amazing his mercurial mate didn't strangle him. "What happened next?" the blond asked as if he were waiting for Cal to tell him a bedtime story.

He swallowed the lump in his throat, certain every pack member there could scent his fear.

"A few nights ago someone broke into our house and drugged us. By the time I woke up, Cindy was gone. They left a note taped to my bedroom door. It said if I wanted to see my sister I had to meet them at an address they wrote down. When I got there it was an abandoned warehouse."

"Why didn't you call the police?" Mikel asked, his eyes narrowing suspiciously. From the constant glares, Cal could see the other vamp didn't like how close Alesandro sat to him.

He shrugged helplessly. "It said not to contact the authorities if I wanted Cindy alive. Frankly, I thought it was some sort of college prank. I mean, who really does that kind of stuff?" He looked around the table but a sea of glares made him hurry on with his tale. "When I got there, it was an empty warehouse with the door propped open. The man who met me stayed in the dark and told me if I brought him Anthony, he would give me my sister back. I think Cindy must've told someone about this contract and they thought it would be the perfect opportunity to get close to Anthony." He gave the architect a small smile. "Sorry."

Anthony shrugged. "If I had any siblings, I'd trade my ass for them too."

As if needing further reassurance, Silver pulled Anthony onto his lap and rubbed his cheek along his mate's, spreading his scent across the other man. Calvin watched in awe to see if Silver would pee a circle around the blond next.

"Why is someone after Anthony?" Alesandro asked.

"The man said you killed his brother," Cal remembered, replaying the discussion in his head.

"Ned," the dark-haired wolf growled, jumping to his feet. "This must be about Ned."

"Sit down, Dillon," Silver ordered. "At least we have some idea what this is about. Now we need to make a plan. We'll get your sister back, Calvin, but we can't rush into this and put Anthony into danger. Sorry."

The alpha didn't look particularly sorry as he sat there cradling his mate. He looked pretty damn content.

Anger coursed through Calvin. "Well I can't just let them keep my sister. She's only twenty and she's in the hands of psychos who don't mind harming women. What do you think they're going to do to her if they think I've changed the rules on them? Killing her would be a mercy when they're done."

Shit, his eyes were welling up.

He gave a yelp as Alesandro pulled him onto his lap. Giving into temptation, he let the other man cuddle him while he pondered the best plan to get his sister back. It might undermine his manliness to discuss war strategy while cuddled up to the vampire, but damn if he didn't like the care and concern oozing from the other man.

Sighing, Calvin snuggled into the embrace and turned to Anthony when he spoke.

"So, what if we let him kidnap me? Someone can follow and rescue me in time."

"No!" the shout rang throughout the room from multiple throats.

"Absolutely not," the large alpha growled.

"But it would make the most sense. If he wants me, then let's give him me. It's not like I can't defend myself."

Silver shook his smaller mate. "But what if he has a gun? I can't chance it, sweetness."

"Are you saying I can't protect myself any better than a twenty-year old girl?"

For the first time, the alpha looked concerned as he watched his small mate as if he were a bomb waiting to detonate. "I can't chance something happening to you."

"You won't. The pack can keep an eye on me the entire time."

The big werewolf paled as his mate

blithely continued. "So it's settled. I'll go and the others can follow. We'll nail this guy."

Silver sighed and nuzzled his mate's neck. "All right, but if anything happens to you I'll never forgive you."

"Understood."

For the first time Alesandro spoke up. "I'll go with Anthony. I can make myself invisible so they won't know I'm accompanying him."

Cal could almost feel the relief in the alpha's stance. "That would be much appreciated, Alesandro," Silver said.

"We'll go, too," Mikel said. Darian nodded.

"No." Alesandro shook his head. "If the guy is a wolf he'll sense it if too many of us go in. As it is he might smell me, but if I mark Calvin first he might just think it's my scent on him. We can't risk Anthony's life. I doubt this man is working alone. You two can follow but stay outside the warehouse. Only Cal, Anthony, and I will go inside."

The other vampires reluctantly agreed. The group sat around and made plans until everyone was satisfied except Silver. Calvin doubted the big alpha would be happy unless the beautiful man went in with a full body suit of armor.

"I don't like this," Silver sulked.

"You'll be close enough to save me if I get into trouble, sweetie. Don't worry so much." Anthony patted Silver's knee, looking unconcerned.

For the first time, Calvin wondered how Anthony killed Ned. It was obvious everyone knew about the other man's death and no one looked particularly sorry for the event. What had Ned done to deserve being killed?

If Calvin thought Silver was like a dog worrying over a bone, he was smart enough not to mention it. The werewolf didn't say anything, but there was a look in the large man's eyes he didn't trust. If anything happened to Anthony he might as well let the blackmailer kill him. It would probably be a more humane way to go than a werewolf mauling.

CHAPTER FOUR

"This is so exciting." Anthony beamed up at Calvin. "I don't mean the part about your sister because I'm sure you're worried, but I've never been part of a sting before. It's not something architects usually get to do. We generally sit at our desk and draw stuff, and sometimes go out to a site."

He bounced alongside Calvin with Alesandro drifting invisibly beside them. Calvin could feel the force of the vampire even if he couldn't see him. Taking a deep breath to steady his nerves, he tried to focus on where they were going. He didn't care what the others said, he had a feeling this wasn't going to be as easy as everyone thought.

Tension tightened his chest. Anyone who went to all that effort to kidnap Anthony wasn't going to just hand over his sister. Not even if he served the blond up on a platter. Of course, if he did that his life wouldn't be worth spit. Silver would rip him to shreds before he could even confess.

The warehouse looked just as old and abandoned as it had the first time. He felt a chill race down his back as he pushed open the creaking metal door. Fear tingled up his spine as they entered the building.

"Hello," he called. For appearances he pulled out a gun and held it to Anthony's head.

"Easy, beautiful. No shooting Anthony," Alesandro's voice whispered into his mind.

He tried to send reassuring messages back but he doubted they left his own mind. Talking telepathically wasn't one of his abilities. Hell, he didn't have any abilities that didn't involve woodworking. He was definitely not the espionage type.

"There you are. I was beginning to think you'd gotten lost," a familiar cold voice wafted across the empty expanse.

With careful steps they crossed the empty warehouse, keeping the gun trained on Anthony as they walked. A small whimper jerked his attention ahead. Cindy sat tied to a chair, a bandana wrapped across her mouth. Her eyes were wide and terrified. He didn't know if she was scared of her psycho kidnapper or her brother holding a gun to a guy's head.

"You'll never get away with this, Calvin," Anthony hissed. "Silver will hunt you down and rip out your heart." The blond said it with such vicious enthusiasm Calvin felt his blood freeze in his veins.

"You won't be around to enjoy his death," the cold voice stated in emotionless tones. "And since the idiotic alpha is convinced you're lifemates, he'll fade at your death and the pack will disband." The man finished with such glee in his voice, Calvin knew this was the ultimate goal. Anthony wasn't the target, Silver was.

"I thought this was about revenge on Anthony?" Calvin said. "You said he killed your brother."

For the first time the man stepped from the shadows. Horror filled Calvin as he got a look at the creature. The man wasn't man nor beast but a scary combination of the two. A long snout extended from the man's face with long fangs curving outwards like the teeth of a boar, while mean yellow eyes watched him with malicious glee. The man/creature wore a long sleeved shirt and loose cargo pants, so they couldn't see what lay beneath the oddly shaped bulges. He was completely certain it was better that he never know. "It's true Anthony killed my brother, but we were only half brothers and I hated the bastard anyway. I want Silver dead and his pretty mate is the perfect way to do it. Once you kill the strongest the others will quickly fall."

"What are you?" Calvin couldn't keep the horror out of his voice. It wasn't only the man's mutation that bothered him; it was the feeling of wrongness that oozed out of him like sickly oil.

"I'm the next generation of wolves," the creature said, walking forward in an odd gait as if his body wasn't put together quite right and his bones and muscles didn't know how to work together. "We're the wolves who don't have to hide what we are in a puny human shell." Saliva dripped from his fangs leaving wet splatters as he walked. "We're the ones who will take over when we get rid of all you stupid humans and the wolves masquerading as you. That's why all the alphas have to go, starting with Silver."

Panic ripped through Calvin. This wasn't a simple kidnapping. This was war. What the hell did he get in the middle of?

A low snickering came from the creature, a hideous sound between a snarl and a chuckle. "As you can see, I've kept my end of the bargain. A wolf is only as good as his word." He nodded towards Anthony. "You'll both have to die, of course, but your sister will be released as I promised. We won't even start hunting her until the next full moon. For ambience you know." He gave a long, coughing laugh. Calvin's distaste of the man rose to an unbearable fury.

A strange crackling filled the air. Calvin stepped away from Anthony as a snap of electricity slapped across his skin.

The creature's head turned towards Anthony. "Say hello to Silver in hell."

From the back of his waistband the mutant pulled a pistol. As Anthony lifted his hand, the creature's pistol cracked. Before Calvin's horrified eyes, a red spot bloomed on Anthony's chest. The pretty blond fell over with a thud.

"Nooo!" Calvin shouted, reaching for Anthony as he fell. Blind with fury he shot at the werewolf but it was too late.

A loud scream pierced the air, ending in a bubby gurgle. He'd forgotten about Alesandro. He looked over in time to see the vampire grab the wolf creature and rip him apart. The sound of wet chunks hitting the ground made his stomach threaten to revolt.

He forced his attention to Anthony. The wolf was dead, but then, so was sweet, gentle Anthony who treated him like a friend even once he knew of Calvin's betrayal. He didn't even look up when he felt Cindy stroke his head.

"I'm sorry about your friend," he heard her say like she was at the end of a long tunnel. Alesandro must have released her.

He felt numb.

Beautiful, loving, Anthony… gone.

"Shhh, my sweet." Alesandro's arms wrapped around Calvin, cradling him in a gentle embrace. "It's not your fault. None of this is your fault."

"It's all my fault, and now Anthony is gone." He could barely talk through the hard knot in his throat.

A mournful howl filled the air. An enormous silver wolf burst through the warehouse door seconds ahead of the rest of the wolf pack. En masse, they filled the cavernous area, forming a large circle around Anthony.

Silver morphed into his human form, the large man falling to his knees in despair. Snatching Anthony from Calvin, the tough alpha clutched his lover, tears dripping down his face.

Blinking back his own tears, Calvin watched as Silver tenderly brushed back his mate's hair from his beautiful face.

The alpha's voice was little more than a shattered whisper. "Come on baby it's time to stop pretending. I know how you love attention but this is over the top even for you. Wake up and show me your beautiful eyes."

A low hum filled the air followed by a pulsing white light. Calvin watched as the brilliant glow shimmered and created a doorway. Once it was fully formed, a man and a woman stepped through. The woman was petite with deep red hair and a tiny figure. She barely came up to the shoulder of the huge guy behind her. The man was all golden skin, muscles, and silvery hair. They both wore simple white robes like Grecian throwbacks.

"What happened to my son?" the woman asked in a voice that made dozens of goose bumps chase themselves up Calvin's arms. The man might look threatening but there was pure magic in the woman's voice.

Silver looked up, tears still streaming from his eyes.

"He was shot. Can you save him?"

"No," the man said. His voice had shadows of power that pulsed across the room with each syllable.

"What do you mean, no?" screamed Silver as he clutched Anthony's still body tighter. You could almost hear his heart break in the silent building.

Anthony's mother elbowed his father in

the stomach. From the man's flinch it wasn't a loving nudge either.

"What my insensitive husband is trying to say is that we don't need to heal Anthony. An hour after his birth, my father-in-law gave Anthony a vial of essence. He's immortal. He can't be killed, especially with something as primitive as a gun. By the way, I'm Hallea, this is my husband Gallien." Anthony's mother spoke with perfect serenity like they were meeting over tea. The fact the alpha didn't rip out her throat probably had more to do with the calming magic she sent out in waves than the alpha's temperament.

"If he can't die, why isn't he waking up?" Silver demanded, completely ignoring the niceties. Any respect Calvin ever had for the alpha just tripled. The werewolf alpha had balls to stand up to the powerful couple who were also his in-laws.

Gallien stepped forward and damned if every single wolf didn't step back a pace. That man was so scary-powerful it pulsed off his body in waves. Unlike Anthony, this man could never pass for human.

The man kneeled on the other side of Anthony and tilted his head towards him. The blond's lifeless eyes looked back.

"My father has taken him away. For the brief moment Anthony was dead, Zeus has the ability to call his soul." Gallien smiled. "Anthony's always been his favorite."

Silver snarled. "Are you saying that while my heart is breaking he's having a chat with his grandfather?"

Hallea sighed, stepping forward. More than one wolf snuck a sniff at her as she walked. Calvin surmised she had the same scent the wolves talked about Anthony having. "My son is powerful, but even he can't escape the clutches of a god. He can't return without Zeus's permission. To even try would be a terrible breach of etiquette." Her forest green eyes met Silver's. "Trust me when I tell you insulting a god is never a good idea."

Gallien looked at his son for a moment. "But neither is staying in one's presence for too long. Zeus is very fond of Anthony, because my son looks almost exactly like him, even if he is a bit shorter. I have a feeling my father would be more than happy to keep Anthony with him for a while." Gallien looked at Silver for the first time. "For a while, in god time, could be centuries. Let me see what I can do." With those words the demigod pressed his hands on either side of Anthony's head. "Father, release my son so he can return to his mate. You know it's against the rules for mates to be parted."

"This will be a good test to see if you're true mates," Hallea said. "He'll have to return him if you're bonded."

"We're true mates." Silver's eyes lit with a feral intensity. Calvin worried for a moment he would lunge at her. Thankfully the wolf was distracted by his mate's movements.

Anthony's body convulsed as light seeped from his pores and streamed out of his mouth like some horrific science fiction movie. Calvin turned away when the light flashed out in blinding brilliance.

When he looked back it was to see the slim blond hugging his mate with such intensity and adoration it was almost painful to witness.

That was what he wanted. Meeting Alesandro's green eyes, he knew he wanted more from the vamp than his lover was willing to give.

With effort he wrenched his eyes away from the vampire. "Come on Cindy. Let's get you home."

In the rush of people clamoring around Anthony, Calvin made his escape, not bothering to look at his lover again. Some scabs were better to rip off before they started to itch.

CHAPTER FIVE

In the end, Cindy couldn't help with information on the mutants. She knew little about her kidnappers. They left her alone when they weren't hitting her and they didn't conveniently tell her where their hideout was located. The only thing she was certain of was that there were four people who kept her captive, but they spoke little so she had no idea where their hideout might be.

Shit.

With no other clues the wolves were on the high alert and Silver continued holding the pack in tight formation.

Calvin didn't recover from the ordeal as quickly as his sister. The shadows under her eyes were starting to fade as well as her bruise, but his were getting darker. He still had shaking nightmares about his sister being captured. The mutant wolves knew where they lived, so he didn't feel safe at night. He installed a security alarm and for the first time in his life kept a gun under his pillow.

* * * *

Alesandro sat at the bar in the new hotel, resting his chin on one hand; his body slumped over the fine-grained wood. It was still uncarved, since Calvin hadn't returned to finish the job. Something neither he nor Anthony was happy about.

A hand slid up his back, patting him in sympathy.

"What's wrong, sweetie?" Anthony's brilliant blond head appeared beside him. He admired the beauty of the man even as he longed for darker hair beside his own at night.

"Calvin is avoiding me."

Sparkling gold eyes watched him with concern. "What makes you think that?"

"He won't return my calls and he doesn't answer the door. Oh, and he avoids me in person."

"I thought the two of you looked pretty close at the warehouse. He's fond of you, sweetheart, I could tell."

"Well your dazzling instincts are wrong. Ever since that night he's avoided me. It's been two weeks."

"Hmmm."

He waited but nothing else was forthcoming.

"That's all you've got?" Alesandro

couldn't stop the bitter laugh coming from his chest even as his heart broke a little. He was hoping Anthony would have some brilliant insight into his problems.

"Maybe your man needs a little wooing."

"Wooing? And I thought I was the old-fashioned one."

Anthony gave one of his famous laughs. "Just because it's an old-fashioned word doesn't mean it doesn't work. I can try to talk to Calvin and find out what the problem is, but it doesn't hurt to weigh things in your favor. Even tough men like to feel appreciated. Maybe he thinks you hold him responsible for my injury."

"We both know it was a mistake that could've gotten you killed, if you could be killed. By the way, the fact you can't die doesn't appear to have appeased your mate."

Anthony gave him a pained grin. "You noticed that, too? Instead Silver keeps going on about my parents and how they must think he doesn't take good care of me. He's talking of doubling my guards."

Alesandro shook his head in amusement. "If you could try and talk to Calvin, that would be great." He felt a little better. It helped to unburden his troubles to a non-vampire friend. His vampire associates weren't much help. Hell, most of them wondered why he was still mooning over a mere human. The rest were of the grab-him-and-make-him-yours mindset, but Calvin was a gentle soul in the body of a god. You treated a treasure like him with the care he deserved.

Ideas bubbled through Alesandro's mind. Yes, he could do that. "You work on the hotel, my friend. I'll work on the wooing."

Anthony laughed again. "You do that, sweet. You do that."

* * * *

The sound of someone moving around in the kitchen drew Calvin from his disturbing dreams, nightmares where Anthony and Alesandro weren't healthy, happy, and living, but instead, dead on the floor.

It was maddening. The same nightmare came to him night after night. In the past two weeks he'd gotten maybe a total of ten hours of sleep. He was starting to feel like the walking dead, except he was pretty certain Alesandro got more sleep than he did. Stumbling into the kitchen he was surprised to find his sister sitting at the kitchen table.

"Can't sleep?"

The hollows under her eyes were fading, but still there.

She shook her head. "They took me while I was sleeping. Every time my eyes close I wonder where I'll wake up."

Shit, he'd thought she was getting better.

Calvin leaned over and gave her a hug. "I know. I worry every time I wake up that you'll be gone, and if I do fall asleep I dream about Anthony being dead. Want some tea?"

Cindy shook her head. "Do we have any more of that cider?"

Opening the fridge, Calvin took a look inside. "Some." He picked up the jug and shook it. "Enough for two." Within minutes he pulled two steaming mugs from the microwave and sat down across from his sister.

"We're quite the pair." He gave a strangled laugh, despair crushing his chest.

"Tell me about Alesandro."

"What?"

Cindy gave him a sad smile. "I could tell there was something between you. Besides, he calls every other day and you always pretend you're not here. Is he some creep I should keep an eye out for? Did he break your heart?"

Calvin shrugged. He'd successfully avoided the topic of Alesandro for weeks now, but if anyone deserved the truth it was his sister. Even though he usually wasn't the type to do heart to heart talks, his sister was the exception to the rule. Between sips of cider, he poured out his experience to his sister, avoiding mentions of hot vampire sex but leaving in everything else. There was such a thing as over sharing, even between close siblings.

Setting her cup down with a clunk, Cindy stared at her brother. "So this vampire puts his life on the line to save me and you've been avoiding him ever since."

Calvin stared at her in shock. "That's what you got out of this story? What about the werewolf and Anthony? They must hate me. I haven't even gone back to the job site. We're probably going to be run out of town for endangering the alpha werewolf's mate."

Cindy laughed, a relief to hear after the tension filled days following her abduction. Calvin wondered if there were any paranatural psychologists he could send her to. Unfortunately, he was pretty certain the people he could ask for advice weren't talking to him. Despite Alesandro's phone calls, he doubted they wanted him around.

"You all survived the encounter, even if it was a bit rough. I survived, you survived, and it's time to take back your life. We can't continue this way, waiting for another one of those creatures to grab us again. There's nothing to say they won't grab you next. I don't know why the one wolf went to the meeting by himself, but I don't doubt the others know he's dead by now and they might be out looking for revenge. We need help, and from the constant phone calls, this vampire you love cares about you."

"I'm not in love." Calvin denied, firming his chin stubbornly and turning away from his sister's probing gaze. "Besides, Alesandro is a sophisticated vampire, how could he love a man who's stupid enough to get put in a situation where he almost gets someone killed. If Anthony wasn't immortal he would be dead."

"He survived, and the vampire is obviously still interested. Is it the vampire thing?" Cindy's brown eyes filled with concern

Calvin shrugged. "I don't mind the vampire thing, but I don't want him because he feels sorry for the poor idiot human who can't save himself."

"Hell, Calvin, you're more of a girl than I am."

Calvin gasped. "You take that back."

"No." Cindy smiled. "Calvin's in love,"

she said in a singsong tone.

He did the only thing a mature older brother could do in this situation. He pounced, knocked her to the ground, and knuckled her hair, giving her a noogie.

Cindy screamed with laughter.

After a few moments he let her up and stomped from the room.

* * * *

Still smiling, Cindy went to retrieve her brother's phone. After years of sacrifice, her big brother deserved to be happy. Scrolling down his missed call list, she picked the one listed with the most incoming calls, but not returned.

"Hello, baby, decided to talk to me, did you?" A seductive voice said on the other end.

Cindy cleared her throat. This definitely didn't sound like someone who felt sorry for her brother or wanted him out of pity. "This isn't Calvin, this is Cindy."

"Where's Calvin. Is he in trouble?" The seductive voice of a moment ago was now crisp and hard.

"No. No. Nothing like that. I wanted to talk to the man my brother's in love with."

"He's in love with me?" Alesandro's

relieved laughter came across the phone. "That does make it easier. Thanks for telling me. I'll take care of everything from here."

The line went dead. For the first time since her capture, Cindy went to sleep with a smile on her face.

CHAPTER SIX

The ringing doorbell woke Calvin out of an uneasy sleep.

Blinking, he barely remembered to slide on a pair of pants before stumbling to the door.

A glance at his alarm clock told him it was barely eight in the morning.

Looking through the peephole he saw a mass of flowers standing on his doorstep. Curious, he opened the door. A strange man stood there holding an enormous bouquet of red tulips, white carnations, and other flowers he didn't recognize with the words 'Flowers by Zeke' emblazoned on his chest.

"Can I help you?"

"Are you Calvin Sanders?"

"Yes."

"Sign here for your flowers."

Still sleep befuddled, Calvin signed and accepted the flowers, looking closely at the arrangement.

"Do you know the language of flowers?"

"What?"

Blinking he looked at the delivery driver again. The man was handsome in that perfect pretty boy style. Not his type. He preferred them tall, dark, and undead.

"The language of flowers. I'm guessing the guy who sent these knew his stuff. He was very specific. We had to look pretty hard to find them this time of year."

Calvin tucked the vase in the crook of his elbow so he could rip open the small florist card.

> *May the flowers tell the secrets of my heart.*
>
> *Yours,*
> *Alesandro*

"What does this bouquet say?" he demanded.

The driver gave him a smirk. "Now you're interested."

"You read the card, didn't you?" he asked with suspicion.

Shrugging, the driver gave him a wide smile. "Someone has to put them in those little envelopes."

"So tell me, what do red tulips say?"

"Red tulips are for perfect love, and the white carnations are for pure love and good luck. These buttery yellow flowers are primroses and they mean 'I can't live without you'. I had to search hard not to get evening primrose because those mean 'inconstancy'. From your bouquet I'd say your guy is trying to tell you he loves you and can't live without you."

A glow of warmth filled Calvin. He couldn't stop the wide smile from spreading across his face. "You think so?"

The driver nodded. "I do. You have a nice day now."

"Wait. I want to give you a tip for your trouble." Calvin pulled his wallet out of his jeans. He'd forgotten to remove it last night when he'd staggered home, exhausted from work. Sometimes laziness came in handy. He pulled out a ten and handed it over.

Laughing the driver took the money and put it in his pocket. "I'm thinking you should go call your boy now and tell him it's reciprocal."

Cal smiled. "I think you're right."

Going inside, he placed the flowers on the counter and grabbed his phone off its charger by the windowsill.

Taking a deep breath he dialed the number he'd memorized by heart.

"Hello." The sound of Alesandro's

sleepy voice made his heart pound as nerves took over and he forgot how to speak.

"Calvin? Baby?"

"Hello." He was an idiot. What kind of person called a vampire first thing in the morning?

"Did you get my flowers?"

"Yes. I'm sorry about calling you. I wasn't thinking."

"You can always call me," the vampire reassured Calvin. "Would you be interested in meeting me tonight?"

He wanted to see Alesandro so badly it hurt. "Where?" He was proud to hear his voice was only a little shaky.

"My place." The vampire rattled off his address, a location in the middle of downtown. "See you at ten."

"I'll be there."

Disconnecting, Calvin slid down the wall to sit on the floor of the kitchen. He hoped the flowers meant what he and the delivery guy thought they did.

* * * *

"Will you stop pacing!" Anthony's irritated tone stopped the vampire in his tracks.

"Sorry. What if he doesn't want me?"

"Then you pull up your big boy pants and get over it because I need him to help me with my project." Anthony flashed him a smile that, for once, Alesandro didn't feel the least compulsion to return. "Oh come on, the kid's face said it all. He wants you, Al, don't believe it if he tells you he doesn't. I think he has other worries. From what you told me he's been shouldering the burden of taking care of his sister by himself since he was really young. He's not used to depending on other people. I think once we clear the air and tell him we don't blame him for the shooting, he'll do better."

"Silver still blames him."

Anthony shrugged. "He'll get over it. At least he let me come over here with only four bodyguards."

Alesandro looked at the four alert werewolves standing at the windows and door. "It is better than six." He didn't mention he'd spotted at least four others on the roof of the building across the street. He didn't want to ruin the tentative truce the alpha and his mate had built.

Their conversation came to a halt when the doorbell rang.

With a look at Anthony, Alesandro went

to answer the door. "Come on in."

Calvin looked tired. There were bags under his eyes and new lines around his mouth that weren't there days before.

He stopped in his tracks when he saw Anthony.

"I-I'm sorry," Calvin said, shifting from side to side and looking anywhere but at the other man.

Anthony walked over and gave the human a hug. "I don't blame you. You couldn't have known he was going to shoot me." The blond stepped back and glared at him. "But I will blame you if you don't come back and finish your job. My bar is pitiful. I didn't drag that dryad's tree hundreds of miles just to slap it on my bar top and leave it that way."

"You still want me?"

Some of the tension ran out of his body at those words.

Anthony gave him a little shake. "Calvin, you are an extremely talented woodworker. I'd be an idiot not to want you on my project. Can I expect to see you next week?"

"Yes, sir." Calvin nodded. "I'll be there bright and early."

"Good." With a cheery wave, Anthony headed out the door, his werewolf retinue following close behind.

The pair of them stood silently staring at each other as the door shut behind Anthony and his werewolves.

"He's a good guy. I don't know if I would've forgiven someone for getting me shot."

Alesandro shrugged. "I'm sure it hurt but he isn't the type to hold a grudge. I'd stay away from Silver for a while, though. I don't think he's recovered yet from seeing his mate shot."

"Will do. He doesn't come to the hotel very often so that shouldn't be too hard."

Alesandro stepped closer to the human. Unable to resist touching the other man he slowly approached and wrapped Calvin in his arms.

"I missed you. When you didn't return my calls I thought I'd lost my chance."

"I didn't want you to date me because you felt sorry for the pitiful human."

The vampire stepped back. "Why would you think that?" he demanded. "There are a lot of feelings I have for you, and not one of them is pity."

Alesandro slid his fingers into Calvin's hair and jerked him closer. Leaning down he pressed his lips against the human's until, with a groan, the other man kissed him back. Unable to stand the separation between them, he stripped them both quickly and efficiently, pleased when he felt the other man was as hard as he was.

"Bedroom," he panted. If he didn't get inside his man soon, he would explode.

Impatient with the human's pace, Alesandro lifted up the muscular woodworker and flipped him over his shoulder. With vampiric speed he reached his bedroom in seconds and laid his lover across his soft sheets.

"I've dreamed of seeing you lying in my bed." It was nothing less than the truth, and the reality was so much better. He frowned as he noticed, once again, the stress on his human's face. "What's bothering you?"

Instead of ravishing Calvin, he felt a compulsive need to listen and see if there was any way he could help. He didn't like to see the other man upset.

"I keep worrying the wolves will return. They know where we live. I… I'd hate for them to take Cindy again. Next week she'll be off at school during the day but at night…"

"You worry."

Calvin nodded.

"I can send some men over to watch her tonight if that will help."

Some of the tension left the human's face.

"Yeah, that would be great."

Alesandro sent a silent message to Darian and got a message in return.

"Darian is on his way."

"I thought he didn't like me?"

"It matters not if he likes you, he wouldn't leave a woman unprotected. He's very traditional that way." Alesandro didn't mention Darian had a little crush on Calvin's sister. No need to worry him further for a completely different reason.

"Now, as for keeping you safe, once you move in with me that won't be a problem."

"Who said I was moving in with you?"

"I did." Alesandro leaned down and kissed his human senseless. When he lifted his mouth there was a dazed look in Calvin's eyes.

Perfect.

* * * *

Calvin didn't know if moving in together was such a good idea, but he couldn't marshal enough thoughts to put up a good argument. Between Alesandro's hands and his amazing mouth, he could barely remember his name.

Without giving him a chance to take a deep breath, the vampire flipped Calvin over onto his stomach, positioning him where Alesandro could get the best angle. He whimpered as a warm tongue lapped at his entrance.

Calvin had never been rimmed before. He thought that was something only done in porn movies and dirty books. He had no idea men did that to each other in real life, or that it felt so fucking amazing.

"Yes, oh yes." He could barely form words as grunts and sighs made up his new vocabulary. "Fuck me," he whispered. There wasn't enough air left in his lungs for fully spoken words.

"Oh, I'm going to," the vampire's rich voice strummed through Calvin's body like a physical touch.

Before he could get his bearings, Alesandro was pressing inside. Groaning, Calvin took a slow breath and relaxed, trying to ease the way of his lover's passage.

"That's right, baby, relax for me. Take all of me," the vampire cooed, sliding slowly into Calvin. "You are so perfect. We're going to fuck like bunnies and then we're going to get your stuff and move you in here. There's an apartment a few floors down we can move you sister into while she's going to school, but we aren't going to leave you alone in that house where those mutant freaks know you live."

Calvin sighed, both from the sensation of his lover pegging him perfectly and the relief of having things taken out of his hands. For once he didn't have to be the strong one. Instead he could lay his troubles on his lover's shoulders and know they would be taken care of.

He should probably object to having his life rearranged, but he was so relieved he could hardly stand it.

"It's okay, baby, everything is going to be all right."

Calvin cried out as Alesandro took him to the edge with powerful strokes. Cum shot from his cock in quick, hot bursts onto the sheets below. He felt the vampire still inside him and wetness fill his ass.

"You are mine." His sex-muddled mind barely deciphered the whisper before sharp teeth pierced his neck, sending him over the edge again in a blissful haze.

Several minutes later, he found himself on his back looking up at his worried lover.

"Am I a vampire now?"

Alesandro laughed. "No. I took a little

too much blood. Combined with the lack of rest you've been getting, you passed out."

The vampire brushed Calvin's hair away from his face in a gentle gesture. "I'm glad you came back to me."

"Yeah, I am too."

"About what I said before. You don't have to move in with me, but I do think it's the best solution to your problem."

Remembering the looks on Alesandro's vampire friends' faces, he had to ask. "And what is your vampire posse going to think about that?"

"They are going to think whatever they want, but they'd better keep any negative words to themselves." There was no mistaking the chill in the vampire's eyes. "You are going to be my mate. One day, if things progress like I hope they will, you will become my vampire partner. Right now, everyone has to stick together. There are things out there we never suspected and, as a community, we will have to fight them as a group. I won't allow dissension in my ranks any more than Silver would allow it in his pack. Vampires are more independent than wolves but we have our own hierarchy too. If you haven't figured it out, I'm in charge of my vampire clan and that makes you the most important person in our small group. My people will learn that not only do they have to tolerate you, but also they have to protect you much like Anthony has werewolves protect him." He lifted Calvin's chin so he was forced to meet his eyes. "You are my everything, Calvin Sanders, and I'd like to be yours if you'll have me."

Calving looked at the gorgeous vampire before him. Sure, they had things that would need ironing out over time and he'd have to watch that Alesandro didn't walk all over him, but it would be nice to share his life with another. To share the burden of taking care of his sister whom he loved but felt inadequate to guide through college life.

"I'd like to be yours too."

Alesandro leaned over and gave Calvin a slow, sweet kiss that quickly morphed into a nuclear meltdown. When he finally lifted his head, Calvin was a puddle of lust.

"I'm looking forward to our years together, my lover."

Calvin smiled back. "So am I."

The End

ALSO BY AMBER KELL:

Available at **Silver Publishing:**

Blood Signs
Xavier's Xmas
Soldier Mine (Sept 17)
Blood Signs 2: Samhain's Kiss (Oct 15)

A WIZARD'S TOUCH
Jaynell's Wolf
Kevin's Alpha (Apr 30)
Kellum's Wizard (Sept 9)

HIDDEN MAGIC
William's House

DRAGONMEN
Mate Hunt (June 25)
Mate Test (July 23)
Mate Dance (Aug 20)

FAE
Heart Connections (Oct 1)

MOON PACK
Attracting Anthony
Baiting Ben
Courting Calvin
Denying Dare
Enticing Elliott
Finding Farro (May 14)

Getting Gabe (May 28)
Hunting Henry (June 11)
Inflaming Inno (July 9)

Available at **Total-E-Bound:**

Hellbourne (May 2)
Taking Care of Charlie (June 20)

COWBOYS
Tyler's Cowboy (Mar 28)
Robert's Rancher (coming soon)

SUPERNATURAL MATES
From Pack to Pride
A Prideful Mate
A Prideless Man (coming soon)

REVIEWS:

Literary Nymphs Reviews gives *Jaynell's Wolf* 5 Nymphs!

Jaynell Marley arrives at Mayell Wizard Academy to complete his training. Jay had already had years of advanced private tutoring, therefore his school enrollment is more to honor his father's wishes. Joining his new dorm roommates for pizza, Jay literally bumps into werekin Thomas Sparks. A sniff at Jay's neck has Thomas proclaiming that Jay is his mate.

Jaynell's Wolf is the first book in the *Wizard's Touch* series. The plot is well written plus vastly entertaining. The main characters are impressive, along with amusing secondary characters. Jaynell is a powerful wizard who wonders why his father insisted that Jay attend a school when it is clear Jay surpasses everyone in magical skills. However, Jay has an unpretentious personality. Thomas is a considerate protector, as long as others keep a respectful distance from Jay. The secondary characters include Gnomes, dragons, half elf, wolf pack in addition to a variety of wizards in training. I thoroughly enjoyed *Jaynell's Wolf*. Amber Kell has created a fantastic flight of the imagination that is laugh-out-loud hilarious, interwoven with heartwarming moments as well as rousing scenes of intimate passion. I look forward to the next addition to the *Wizard's*

Touch series.

* * * *

Lisa at Joyfully Reviewed — "*Blood Signs* is captivating"

"Deliciously dark at times and delightfully wicked as well, ***Blood Signs*** is pure entertainment… [T]he plot will hold you, the characters are engaging, and ***Blood Signs*** is hard to put down once you start. ***Blood Signs*** is captivating.